# SUIC

# RUN

*Depth Force Thrillers*
*Book Eight*

# Irving A Greenfield

SAPERE
BOOKS

# SUICIDE
# RUN

Published by Sapere Books.

24 Trafalgar Road, Ilkley, LS29 8HH,
United Kingdom

saperebooks.com

ISBN: 978-1-80055-887-8

## DEATH FROM ABOVE

*"Can we surface?"* Boxer asked.

*"With decks awash — if there's no wind,"* Cowly answered. *"Otherwise…"*

*"Roger that,"* Boxer said angrily and rubbed his hand over his beard. *Sweat wet his brow and skidded down his back. He could feel the sides of the ship closing in on him. He forced himself to concentrate on the decision he had to make.*

*If he opened the deck hatches, tons of water could come pouring into the* Barracuda. *If he waited …* but he couldn't wait. *He forced saliva into his mouth.*

*"Deck detail,"* he said over the MC. *"Topside through hatches two and three!"*

*Moments later, the hatches were thrown open…*

# CHAPTER 1

From the sail's bridge, Admiral Jack Boxer watched the rubber assault boats pull away from the beach of the Yemen Democratic Republic, ending Russia's attempt to take complete control of that mideastern nation. Each assault boat held twenty men. There were five American assault boats and five Russian. Ten armed Americans accompanied ten unarmed Russians. To keep the Russian assault force from being destroyed by American aircraft, Admiral Igor Borodine had agreed to the arrangement.

Boxer turned to Cowly, his executive officer, and commented, "Those boats are going to have one hell of a time crossing the line of surf."

Cowly nodded and pointing to the two squadrons of F20s overhead he asked, "When do they leave?"

"As soon as the men are aboard," Boxer answered. He glanced at COMMAND COMPUTER'S real time clock. "Twenty minutes should do it."

Cowly looked off to the southeast, where black smoke from the Russian carriers *Minsk* and *Kiev* stained an otherwise cloudless blue sky. "At least we don't have to worry about any Russian aircraft," he said.

"Only a couple of cruisers and probably a couple of attack subs," Boxer answered flatly.

"And the *Sea Dragon*," Cowly said, looking straight at Boxer.

"Only after we return its assault team."

The communications officer keyed Boxer. "Skipper, headquarters demands to speak to you."

"Tysin or Mason?"

7

"Both."

"Patch the call through," Boxer said.

"Ten-four," the COMMO answered.

A moment later Tysin said, "Boxer what the hell is happening there?"

"Nothing now," Boxer said. "The assault force is returning to the *Barracuda*."

"What the hell happened to the Russian force?" Mason shouted.

"The *Minsk* and *Kiev* are dead in the water and still burning and one attack sub is —"

"The assault force?" Mason roared.

"I'm waiting for it to come aboard the *Barracuda*," Boxer said calmly. "It should be here in approximately seventeen minutes."

For several moments neither Mason or Tysin spoke. Then Tysin said, "You will sail to our base in the Seychelles and turn the Russians over to the base commander."

"Negative," Boxer responded.

"What?"

"Negative," Boxer repeated; then added, "As soon as it's possible, the entire Russian assault team will be turned over to Admiral Borodine. That was part of the surrender agreement."

Again there was silence.

"This is Admiral Mason," Mason said. "I —"

Boxer cut the transmission and keyed the COMMO. "Wait two minutes; then radio headquarters and tell them we're having transmission difficulties... Tell them we're in the midst of an electrical storm."

"Aye, aye, Skipper," the COMMO answered.

"They could check that out with the flight leader," Cowly said.

"Probably will," Boxer responded; then wiping his brow with a handkerchief, he commented on the heat.

"The thermometer on the COMCOMP reads ninety-five."

Boxer shook his head. "You could fry an egg on the deck... There's not a hint of a breeze."

"I'll be damned happy when we're under way again," Cowly said.

Suddenly Captain Riggs keyed Boxer. "Skipper, we're approaching the surf."

"Roger that," Boxer answered. He could hear the boom of the breaking waves in the background.

"Stand by to pick us up."

"Roger that," Boxer said and keyed the engineering officer. "Give me sixteen hundred rpms."

"Sixteen hundred rpms," the EO responded.

"Mahony," Boxer called to the helmsman, "take her in as close as you can."

"Aye, aye, Skipper," Mahony responded.

Boxer sucked in his breath and slowly exhaled... Crossing that line of surf in those flimsy assault boats was in his opinion far more dangerous than the attacks he had launched against the Russian carriers.

"Skipper," Mahony said in a quiet voice, "we've got two-zero feet of water under us."

Boxer keyed the EO. "Reduce speed to six hundred rpms."

"Reducing speed to six hundred rpms," the EO answered.

Boxer strained to see through the mist of the breaking surf. "They should be coming out of it by now," he said.

"Should be," Cowly agreed.

The COMMO keyed Boxer. "Skipper, we just received word on an open frequency from the National Earthquake Center in Washington... There's been a major undersea quake at one

zero degrees north latitude, one zero degrees east longitude…
All shipping in a radius of a thousand miles from the quake's epicenter have been warned to expect tsunamic waves. Wave speed two hundred miles an hour."

"Boat, zero five degrees off the starb'd bow," one of the bridge lookouts called.

Boxer keyed the EO. "Stop all engines."

"All engines stopped," the EO responded.

The *Barracuda* began to lose headway.

Boxer switched on the MC. "Deck detail topside, on the double!"

The COMMO keyed Boxer. "Admiral Borodine —"

"Patch him through," Boxer responded.

"Jack," Borodine said, "have you received word of the tsunami?"

"Yes… Just a few moments ago… The assault boats are coming through the line of surf," Boxer explained.

"That wave is moving at two hundred and twenty knots," Borodine said, "and is almost five hundred miles long."

"Christ!" Boxer exclaimed.

"We're in its path. It's less than three-zero minutes from here."

"Roger that," Boxer answered.

"Boat number two one-zero degrees off starb'd bow," a second lookout called.

"Retrieving assault craft," Boxer said. "Will communicate with you as soon as possible."

"Roger that," Borodine answered.

"Boat coming alongside," the chief of the deck detail reported.

Colonel Lyle Dawson was standing in the stern, ready to leap aboard the *Barracuda*.

"That son-of-a-bitch wants out first," Boxer fumed and switching on the MC, he said, "Now hear this… All returning assault troops, now hear this… This is the captain speaking… Officers will remain in the assault craft until all other personnel are aboard the *Barracuda*… I repeat, all officers will remain in the assault craft until all other personnel are aboard the *Barracuda*."

Cowly looked at him and grinned.

One of the lookouts reported a third and fourth boat.

The COMMO keyed Boxer. "Skipper, Sky Chief leader requests permission to speak to you."

"Roger that," Boxer said. "Patch him through."

"Admiral, one of your boats turned over," Sky Chief leader said in a slow western drawl. "Comin' around for a looksee."

Boxer glanced up. Three of the jets turned off to the right and making a tight turn, swooped low over the water.

"Can't even see the boat any more," the Sky Chief leader said.

"Roger that," Boxer responded.

Four more boats were reported by the deck chief.

"Riggs hasn't come in yet," Boxer said.

"I know," Cowly answered. "I've been looking for him."

Boxer switched on the MC. "Colonel Dawson report to the bridge with your Russian counterpart."

The jets made another low level pass and once again the Sky Chief leader reported, "Nothing but white water."

"Roger that," Boxer said. "And thanks for saving our ass."

"Glad to do it," the Sky Chief leader said.

"Nine boats returned," Cowly reported. "The assault force is below and the Russians are in the mess area."

Boxer looked toward the line of surf and shook his head. "Riggs ever talk about his family to you?"

"Married two years ago," Cowly said.

"Any children?"

"They were trying," Cowly replied. "His wife is a high fashion model."

Dawson and the Russian officer came up on the bridge. Lyle Dawson was a lean, muscular man in his early fifties, with graying hair and black eyes.

Looking at Dawson, he asked, "Did you see Riggs's boat go over?"

Dawson shook his head.

Boxer turned his attention to the Russian officer, a short, barrel-chested man. "I am Admiral Boxer, captain of the *Barracuda*."

"Major Georgi Khmyz," the Russian answered, coming to attention and saluting.

Boxer returned the courtesy; then said, "In a short time you and your men will be returned to the *Sea Dragon*... But until that time, I expect you and your men to remain in the area assigned to you and to cause no difficulties... Your men may have food and drink, but they must remain in the assigned area... Any man out of that area will be shot... The only exceptions will be those men who are wounded and they will be under guard in the sick bay area."

"Understood," Khmyz answered.

"Have either of you any questions?" Boxer asked. He expected Dawson to object to returning the Russian assault force to the *Sea Dragon*. But to his surprise, Dawson remained silent.

"Are there toilet facilities in the mess area?" Khmyz asked.

"Nearby... Your men will be escorted to and from them," Boxer said.

Khmyz nodded.

"Dawson," Boxer said, "make sure your men and our Russian guests have what they need."

"Aye, aye, sir," Dawson answered.

Suddenly one of the lookouts reported, "Two men, one-five degrees off port bow."

Boxer moved to the port side.

"Just this side of the surf line, Skipper," the lookout said.

The harsh glare of the water forced Boxer to squint.

"I see them," Cowly said. "I see them!"

Boxer switched on the MC. "Rescue team on deck… Rescue team on deck… Now hear this, rescue team on deck." He squinted at the water again. This time he saw the two bobbing figures and estimated they were two, maybe three hundred yards away.

A four-man rescue team appeared on deck.

"Two swimmers one-five degrees off the port bow, about two to three hundred yards from us."

The four men went into the water and struck out toward the swimmers.

Boxer trained the infra-red glasses on the two men, but couldn't ID either of them. He stepped aside and told Cowly to look. "Maybe you can tell who they are."

"Can't," Cowly said after peering into the glasses for several moments.

Suddenly the COMMO keyed Boxer. "Skipper, we just had another transmission from Washington… There's been a second undersea earthquake a hundred miles southeast of us and another tsunami is heading toward us at a speed of three hundred miles an hour."

"Roger that," Boxer answered, watching the rescue team make its way toward the swimmers. He switched on a special radio and began to vector the rescue team directly toward the swimmers.

The COMMO keyed Boxer again. "Skipper, Admiral Borodine requests permission to speak to you."

"Patch him through," Boxer responded.

"Aye, aye, Skipper," the COMMO said.

"Jack, there's a second tsunami coming toward us at two hundred and eighty knots," Borodine said.

"Roger that," Boxer answered. "We're standing by to pick up two men from the beach… One boat foundered coming through the surf."

"How many lost?"

"All, except the two — our rescue team just reached them… We'll be underway in a few minutes."

"Make it quick, Jack; there are two killer waves out here," Borodine said.

"Roger that," Boxer answered, watching the six men in the water.

"I still can't make out the survivors," Cowly commented, peering through the infra-red glasses.

The COMMO keyed Boxer. "Skipper, Sky Chief leader requests permission to speak to you."

"Patch him through," Boxer said.

"Admiral, we've got to leave you now," the Sky Chief leader said. "We've got to have lunch."

"Roger that," Boxer answered, knowing that "lunch" was the code word for the refueling operation that would enable them to fly back to their base. "And again thanks."

"Glad to help!" the man answered.

The planes came around in a wide circle, swooped low over the *Barracuda* and then, climbing, headed northwest.

"Two of my men," Khmyz said. "I can tell from their uniforms."

Boxer nodded. Though he hoped one of the men would be Riggs, he congratulated Khmyz.

"Thank you, Comrade Admiral," Khmyz said. "Neither I or my men will forget what you did."

"Your Comrade Admiral Borodine would have done the same thing," Boxer answered.

Khmyz grinned, nodded and offering his hand, he said, "I hope some day I can return the favor."

"Let's hope that the next time we meet it will be to drink vodka," Boxer said, shaking Khmyz's hand; then switching on the MC, he ordered the deck detail topside to aid the rescue operation.

As soon as the men on deck were safely below, Boxer turned to Dawson. "Escort Major Khmyz to the mess area."

"Aye, aye, Admiral," Dawson answered and asked Khmyz to follow him down through the hatchway.

"You can bet Dawson is going to make a full report to Tysin," Cowly said. "You killed his dreams of returning to the States a hero."

"Hero?"

"Sure… Standing in front of the video cameras as he tells how he captured all those big, bad Russian assault troops… It sure would make him look good and open all sorts of doors to him in Washington. He might have had a chance at a seat in the House or in the Senate."

"You're joking!" Boxer exclaimed.

"The man is a political animal," Cowly said, "and where would a political animal be happiest?"

"Hero, shit!" Boxer exclaimed, spitting over the side of the bridge. Then switching on the MC, he said, "Now hear this…

All hands now hear this… Prepare to get underway… Prepare to get underway." He turned to Mahony. "How much water do we have under us?"

"Two-two feet, Skipper," Mahony answered.

Boxer keyed the EO. "Reverse at two thousand rpms"

"Reversing at two thousand rpms," the EO said.

The *Barracuda* shuddered and slowly eased backward.

Boxer switched on the MINICOMCOMP's fathometer. "Reading three-zero feet," he said.

"Three-zero feet," Mahony echoed, looking at the Electronic Helm Control.

The COMMO keyed Boxer, "Skipper, Admiral Mason demands to speak to you."

"Patch him through," Boxer answered; then called out a bottom of five-zero feet.

"Five-zero feet," Mahony said.

"Boxer what the hell is your status?"

"Operational," Boxer responded.

"What about those waves?" Mason asked.

"Reading nine-five feet," Boxer said.

"Nine-five feet," Mahony repeated.

"Boxer what are you doing about the waves?" Mason shouted.

"The only thing I can do is —"

"The consensus back here is to try and end run to the west of the wave," Mason said. "From where you are to the end of the wave is two hundred nautical miles… You should be able to —"

"One-two-five feet," Boxer said.

"One-two-five feet," Mahony reported.

"Mason," Boxer said, "tell your consensus to take a flying leap… I'll radio when we're on the other side of the wave."

"You can't go through a wall of water," Mason screamed. "You'll founder."

"Our only chance is to go under it," Boxer said. "Out." And shaking his head, he turned to Cowly. "I never figured Chi-Chi to be the nervous type, did you?"

"Not the Chi-Chi I knew," Cowly replied.

Boxer checked the fathometer and called out, "One-two-five feet."

"One-two-five feet," Mahony said.

Boxer keyed the EO. "Switch to forward drive… Go to twenty knots."

"Switching to forward drive… Going to twenty knots."

"Mahony, come to nine-zero degrees," Boxer said.

"Coming to nine-zero degrees," Mahony replied.

Boxer looked out over the sea. It looked like a polished mirror. "Couldn't guess what was coming our way just by looking at the surface," he commented.

"No way," Cowly agreed.

Boxer struck the klaxon twice, dropped down the hatchway and immediately went to the COMCOMP. The air-conditioned environment was a welcome change from the blistering heat of the sail's bridge. He ran a SYSCHEK. All systems were green. "Lower sail," he said.

"Sail lowered," Cowly answered.

Boxer keyed the diving officer. "Make one hundred feet."

"Making one hundred feet," the DO responded.

The sound of hissing air filled the *Barracuda* as the ballast tanks flooded.

Boxer watched the Digital Depth Read Out. The *Barracuda* was descending at a normal rate. He moved his eyes across the instrument panel. "Usually there's more than one wave," he said. "Sometimes they're close together and sometimes they're separated from each other by several minutes."

"Those Russian carriers are going to have a rough time," Cowly commented.

"A very rough time," Boxer said. "They could very well find themselves part of the beach." He switched on the Under Water Imaging System. Two huge sharks came into view and quickly vanished into the dark blue of the water. "Mean looking mothers," he muttered to himself.

The DO keyed Boxer, "Skipper, one hundred feet."

"Roger that," Boxer said, checking the DDRO and the large depth gauge on the bulkhead, above the COMCOMP. The two registered a depth of one hundred feet. He moved his eyes back to the UWIS. A large octopus was off to the right of the screen... Then suddenly out of the corner of his left eye he caught the momentary flicker of a red light. Instantly he scanned that section of the COMCOMP. All warning lights were out. He ran a SYSCHEK: all systems were green. He keyed the damage control officer. "Run a SYSCHEK," he said.

"Aye, aye, Skipper," the DCO answered.

Boxer looked at the UWIS again. The blue was several shades darker. He could even see some brown in it.

The DCO keyed him. "Skipper, all systems are green."

"Roger that," Boxer answered, aware that he was sweating and his heart was racing. He was about to tell Cowly to take the CONN when the bow was suddenly thrust up. Reflexively, he switched to Automatic Control and went to flank speed.

The bow came down.

"What the hell was that?" Cowly asked.

Boxer shook his head and switched on the MC. "All section chiefs report any injuries to the EXO," he said. An instant later the bow went up again… At flank speed and with water in her ballast tanks, the *Barracuda* was straining toward the surface.

Boxer dialed in a fifteen degree pitch on the bow and stern diving planes; then he completely flooded the bow ballast tanks.

The bow eased down slightly, but they were still heading toward the surface.

"We get caught anywhere near the crest of those waves and we'll be on the beach in a matter of minutes," Boxer said, flooding all the ballast tanks.

"No injuries," Cowly reported.

"We're going for the bottom," Boxer said.

A shudder passed through the *Barracuda*. For several moments, she hung suspended at a depth of seventy-five feet. Then her bow began to settle and pitch downward.

Boxer checked the depth gauge: they were down one hundred and thirty feet. He looked at the fathometer. The bottom was still two hundred and twenty feet below them.

The sonar officer keyed Boxer. "Multiple targets nine-zero degrees… Range twenty-five thousand yards… Speed two-hundred and fifty knots."

"Roger that," Boxer answered and switched on the MC. "All hands, rig for collision… Rig for collision!" The tsunami was moving the debris on the bottom… The sand, the rocks and boulders had been lifted up and were being carried by the incredible force of the surging sea… Boxer braced himself against the COMCOMP.

The DO keyed him. "Can't make bottom, Skipper."

"Roger that," Boxer said, his eyes going to the Dive Control portion of the COMCOMP. All ballast tanks were full and the diving planes were at their maximum angle. He checked the ship's speed: it too was at maximum. Suddenly something slammed into the hull. "A rock," he said, glancing back at Cowly.

"That sounded like a sledgehammer," Cowly commented.

Boxer looked at the UWIS. The screen was filled with dark brown. Nothing was definable.

Two more rocks crashed into the ship's hull.

The DCO keyed Boxer. "Skipper, those last two caused some pressure set."

"What's the condition now?" Boxer said.

"Still hard," the DCO said.

A boulder crashed into the *Barracuda*'s bow. A shudder traveled the length of the ship. Several red lights began to flash on the COMCOMP.

The forward torpedo room officer keyed Boxer. "Two men injured and we're taking water... Several lines ruptured."

"Roger that," Boxer said.

The DCO keyed Boxer. "Damage control party on the way to forward torpedo room."

Boxer acknowledged the DCO's report and keyed the sick bay. "Medics to the forward torpedo room," he said.

"Aye, aye, Skipper," the medical officer responded.

Boxer looked at the flashing red lights. The high-pressure air system was out, and the computer information feed line to the torpedo pre-firing check system was cut.

The DCO keyed Boxer. "Deck bow plates breached... Can be —"

Another boulder crashed into the *Barracuda* and thundered along the length of the deck; then abruptly stopped.

Water spurted from the overhead into the bridge area.

"Skipper," the DCO said, over the still-open key, "main water line is ruptured... Deck plates buckled... Severe danger from short circuiting."

"Roger that," Boxer replied.

"Turning off fresh water pumps," the DCO said.

"Roger that," Boxer answered.

"We stay here, Skipper," Cowly said, "and one of those boulders is going to open us up."

"We tried for the surface and couldn't make it," Boxer told him.

Several more rocks slammed against the outside hull.

The SO keyed Boxer. "Skipper, we're losing headway... We're being pushed back toward the beach."

"Christ!" Boxer swore; then he asked, "How fast?"

"Can't exactly tell... But the beach is now only five thousand yards from our stern."

"What's the speed of the wave?"

"Dropped off to nine-zero knots."

"Roger that," Boxer said. He switched on the MC. "All hands... All hands now hear this... Stand by to surface... Stand by to surface..." He dialed in a new position for the diving planes. The ship responded, tilting bow up. He looked at Cowly for a moment and said, "Maybe near the surface the wave will not be as fast." Then he blew all ballast tanks.

The *Barracuda* seemed to leap up.

Boxer watched the depth gauge above the COMCOMP. They were going up very fast.

The SO keyed Boxer. "Skipper, wave speed down to five-five knots."

"Roger that," Boxer answered and related the information to Cowly. "Five-zero feet to surface," Boxer announced, reducing the angle of the diving planes. He scanned the current indicator. The needle was still off the dial.

The DCO keyed Boxer, "Skipper, there's an additional three tons on the ship."

"What?"

"I've got additional three tons centered on the bridge," the DCO answered.

"Can we surface with it?"

"With decks awash."

"How much —"

"Zero-six to zero-nine inches above the water, if there's no wind," the DCO said.

"Roger that," Boxer answered angrily. Then to Cowly he said, "We've picked up three tons."

"That last boulder?"

"Probably... It's sitting on the sail," Boxer said. "If no sea is running we'll have zero-six to zero-nine inches between our deck and the water."

Cowly shook his head but remained silent.

Boxer switched on the MC. "Deck detail stand by." He watched the depth gauge; they were ten feet down. His eyes went to the current indicator. The needle was back on the dial and showed a fifteen-knot current, moving toward the shore. He looked back at the depth gauge. "Surface... Surface," he announced over the MC. He reduced the speed of the *Barracuda* to twenty-five knots; then to twenty... Against a fifteen-knot current, the *Barracuda* would only be making five knots. Slow enough to take a look at the damage under ordinary circumstances, but these were not in the least bit ordinary.

The DCO keyed Boxer. "That weight is causing the sail to push against the bottom of its well... Pressure is already two-two percent above its acceptable tolerance."

"Any structural deformation?"

"Not yet," the DCO answered. "But metal gets tired, Skipper. And we've got a main joint between the keel and ribs right below."

"Roger that," Boxer said and rubbing his hand over his beard, he could feel the sides of the ship closing in on him. Sweat wet his brow and skidded down his back. He fought down the desire to bolt from the chair and throw open the hatch himself. He needed space around him; he needed fresh air. He forced himself to concentrate on the decision he had to make. If he opened the deck hatches, tons of water could come pouring into the *Barracuda* and cause further damage. If he waited, that three tons could cause structural damage to the hull and — he had to act. He forced saliva into his mouth. "Deck detail," Boxer said over the MC, "topside through hatches two and three… DCO topside." Then he told Cowly to take the CONN.

The hatches were thrown open. Some water splashed down into the *Barracuda*.

Scrambling up through the hatchway, Boxer filled his lungs with fresh air. Then he looked at the deck: it was more than a foot above the sea. He turned toward the sail. A huge boulder was lodged in the bridge.

"Will you look at the size of that mother!" the DCO exclaimed, coming up behind him. His name was Christopher Bond. He was a bald-headed man of middling height, with a long, almost sad face.

"We've got to get it the fuck off," Boxer growled.

"Jackhammers will take it apart."

"Take too long," Boxer said. "It's got to be blasted off." He turned toward the bow. "Those plates have to be welded back in place."

"Skipper, if we blow that sucker apart we're going to put a great deal of strain on that main joint."

Boxer looked at the boulder. It was dark brown, with jagged edges. "We can't dive with that sitting on us," he said and tilting his head up, he added, "and we can't protect ourselves from aircraft without having our radar operational and our radar can't be operational unless the sail is up." He looked at the DCO. "And the sail isn't up because that fucking boulder is sitting on it."

"Aye, aye, Skipper," Bond answered and keying the Damage Control Center he asked for a welding detail and demolitions expert to come topside. Then he went forward to inspect the damage to the bow plates.

"How long will it take to repair the plates?" Boxer asked.

"Four, five hours," Bond said.

Boxer walked to the bow.

"Part of the time we'll have to be dead in the water," Bond told him.

"How long?"

"Won't know until I have a look at the damage," Bond answered.

The welding detail came up on deck, followed by the demolitions expert.

"Try to do it as quickly as possible," Boxer said. "If we're attacked, we wouldn't stand a snowball's chance in hell of surviving."

Bond nodded and took a few moments to tell his men what he wanted done. "When you're ready to inspect the plates below the water line let me know."

"Aye, aye, Chris," the senior rate answered.

Bond turned toward the demo man. "Wicks, can you blow that sucker?" he asked.

The demo man smiled. He was a tall, lanky man with a freckled face, and dark blond hair that verged on being light brown, and green eyes.

"No sweat," Wicks replied.

"Can you blow it apart piece by piece?" Boxer asked.

Wicks looked back at the boulder. "Maybe, but I'd have to set off a couple of charges to see how it breaks up."

"Do it now," Boxer said.

"Aye, aye, Skipper," Wicks responded and turning, he dropped down the hatchway to get his drill and explosives.

"What's the situation below?" Boxer asked, looking at the DCO.

"Repairs are underway... Once the plates in the bow are sealed, we won't be taking on any water and as for the other damage, it's being repaired. The fresh water system should be operational in about an hour."

Boxer nodded. Despite the fact that they were underway, the heat was fierce. He moved closer to the boulder.

Chris followed him.

Boxer balled his fist and smashed it down on the boulder. It reminded him of the enormous dark weight he carried in his head. A weight whose shifting mass could make his heart race, make him sweat and make him afraid...

The COMMO keyed him. "Skipper, Admiral Borodine requests permission to speak to you."

"Patch him through."

"Aye, aye, Skipper," the COMMO answered.

"Jack, that second tsunami is less than five-zero miles from me," Borodine said. "How close are you to the beach?"

"Less than three-zero miles."

"Move further out to sea," Borodine counseled. "I took the first tsunami on the surface. But I'm nine-five miles out to sea."

Boxer said nothing. He regretted having tried to take the *Barracuda* under the waves.

"Jack, do you copy?"

"Copying," Boxer answered, aware that the conversation was taking place over an open channel and was being monitored by every Russian ship within a thousand miles and by anyone else who happened to be tuned to that particular frequency.

"Head out to sea," Borodine said.

"Roger that," Boxer responded.

"Can you confirm rendezvous point and time?" Borodine asked.

"Negative," Boxer said. "Will radio place and time."

"Roger that," Borodine answered, ending the conversation.

Boxer pursed his lips. He wasn't about to say anything about the damage the *Barracuda* had sustained, nor was he going to give the Russian subs and surface ships any hint of where he would transfer Borodine's men back to the *Sea Dragon*. That operation was strictly between him and Borodine.

Wicks came back on deck. "Ready to go," he said.

Boxer nodded.

"I'll set two small charges," Wicks explained. "One about six inches from the top and the second in the exposed part of the bottom. Hopefully that will give us some idea of how it will fracture."

"Go to it!" Boxer said.

Wicks picked up his portable drill and began working on the base.

Boxer started for the bow, when the COMMO keyed him. "Skipper, headquarters is on a priority eight call."

"Patch it through," Boxer said.

Mason came on. "What's your status?"

"As of now we're less than five-zero percent operational," Boxer said. "We have bow damage, which is being repaired and there's a three-ton boulder on top of our sail."

"What the hell is a boulder doing there?"

Boxer shook his head and flippantly answered, "I guess it thought it found a home. But we're doing our best to make it go away."

Tysin came on. "Were all your men safely evacuated?"

"Negative… We lost one boat… Captain Riggs and nine other men are missing and presumed dead."

"I thought you were able to pick up —"

"We picked up two of the Russians who were in the boat that turned over."

"Colonel Dawson —"

"Returned safely," Boxer said.

"Skipper," Wicks called, "ready to blow."

"Stand by," Boxer told Tysin; then to Wicks, he said, "Blow it!"

"Aye, aye, Skipper," Wicks answered and scrambled forward. "Now," he said, pressing the red button on a radio-controlled detonating device.

The two explosions merged and sounded like large firecrackers.

"What the hell was that?" Tysin asked.

"Stand by," Boxer said again, as Wicks ran to see how the boulder fractured.

"Nice, Skipper," Wicks called out. "Real nice. She fractures in slabs… I can blow it apart in manageable pieces."

"How long to do the job?"

"Thirty, maybe forty minutes."

"It's all yours," Boxer said.

"Aye, aye, Skipper," Wicks answered.

Boxer gave his attention back to Tysin and said, "We should be heading into the second tsunami in a matter of minutes."

"Was that an explosion I heard?" Tysin asked.

"We're blowing apart a boulder that rolled onto the sail's bridge. Once it's gone our operational status will increase to nine-zero percent."

"Your orders are to —"

"I know what my orders are," Boxer said, "and I will follow them as soon as I return the Russian assault force to the *Sea Dragon*."

Mason came on. "I could remove you from command," he threatened.

"You could, but you won't… At least not now… Listen and try to understand that the deal I made with Admiral Borodine saved lives; the lives of our own men."

"And the lives of the men in the Russian assault force," Tysin said.

"You've got to give something to get something," Boxer answered.

"From the way we see it," Mason said, "you're giving too damn much."

Boxer wanted to say, "That's because you're blind, Chi-Chi Mason." But instead he uttered a weary sigh and said, "Admiral, when I return, you take whatever action you see fit, but I will return those men to the *Sea Dragon*… Out." And just as he cut the transmission, Wicks blew off another section of the boulder.

"Skipper," Chris said, stepping alongside of Boxer, "can we reduce speed a bit? The men are taking a lot of spray."

Boxer looked toward the bow. The *Barracuda*'s bow was creating a spectrum-colored fan-like curtain on either side of it. "When did that start?" he asked.

"Three, four minutes ago."

Boxer looked at the sea on either side of the ship. Its color had changed from a dark blue to a fuzzy brown. He keyed the SO. "How much water do we have under us?"

"Two-five-zero feet," the SO answered.

"Can you give a distance reading between us and where the bottom starts up toward the beach?"

"No, Skipper, it's out of range."

"Roger that," Boxer answered.

"Stand by," Wicks called out and ran back to where Boxer and the DCO was standing to detonate the explosive charge.

The explosion separated another slab from the main mass of the boulder.

Wicks and several of the men from the deck detail heaved the slab over the side.

"I think we're moving through one of the tsunamic waves," Boxer said.

"Where the hell is it?"

"Most of it, luckily, is under us," Boxer answered. "But I sure as hell wouldn't want to be anywhere near that beach when it hits."

The COMMO keyed Boxer. "Skipper, there's a hell of a lot of Russian traffic."

"How much more?"

"Five-zero percent in the last few minutes," the COMMO answered. "And all of it high priority."

"Can you get fix on either sender?"

"One sender has to be either the *Minsk* or *Kiev*," the COMMO explained, "and there are four other senders, each at different places and all within six-zero to eight-zero miles of us."

"Relay the four positions to the SO and RO."

"Aye, aye, Skipper," the SO answered.

Boxer ran his hand over his beard. He was sure that one of the four senders had to be the *Sea Dragon* and the other three were most probably the two cruisers *Moskva* and *Leningrad* and one of the attack submarines, or two of the attack submarines and one of the cruisers.

Wicks signaled another blow off.

As soon as the slab went over the side, there was perceptible upward movement of the *Barracuda*.

"That must have gained us a few inches," Chris said and called to the rate to see if he noticed any difference.

"We're up about zero-three to zero-four inches," the man answered.

Chris looked at Boxer. "Now all we have to worry about is how much damage that sucker did."

"And the Russians are hunting for us," Boxer said.

"Yeah... I guess I wanted to forget about them," Chris responded.

"I sure as hell can't blame you for that," Boxer told him.

Cowly keyed Boxer. "Skipper, the fresh water system is operational."

"Roger that," Boxer said and relayed the information to Chris.

"I'll go below and see how the other repairs are coming along," Chris told him.

Boxer nodded. He wanted to go below to get away from the heat, but the idea of being inside the *Barracuda* was something he wanted to avoid until it was absolutely necessary for him to be at the COMCOMP.

By the time Wicks blew away half the boulder, the two multi-colored fans of water on either side of the *Barracuda*'s bow diminished to the normal bow wave and the sea became dark blue again.

"Skipper," the rate said, "we're goin' to have to put a man down to check the rest of the bow plates."

"How soon?"

"Like to do it as soon as possible," the man said.

Boxer nodded, keyed the DCO and told him what the situation was.

"I'll send up two sets of scuba gear," the DCO answered; then he added, "HP Air SYS will be operational in a matter of minutes and all breaks in the electrical cables have been repaired."

"Roger that," Boxer said and then keying the EO, he ordered "all engines stopped."

"Stopping all engines," the EO responded.

After a few minutes, the *Barracuda* began to lose headway and eventually she lay dead in the water.

A two-man repair team went over the side, while a four-man anti-shark detail armed with high-powered rifles stood watch on the deck. All of the underwater damage was located just aft on the star'b'd torpedo doors and in forty minutes the *Barracuda* was underway again.

During that time, Wicks blew away all but a few hundred pounds of the boulder and he and the men working with him managed to wrestle that over the side.

"Damn good job," Boxer told Wicks. "Damn good!"

"Piece of cake, Skipper," Wicks answered and went below.

Boxer keyed Cowly. "Stand by to raise sail."

"Standing by."

"Run a SYSCHEK," Boxer said.

"SYSCHEK run… All systems green."

"Raise sail," Boxer said.

"Raising sail," Cowly answered.

The sail came up easily.

Boxer quickly climbed the port side ladder to the sail's bridge. He keyed the RO. "Test all radar," he said.

"Aye, aye, Skipper," the RO answered.

Boxer keyed Cowly again. "For the next one-zero minutes I'll take the CONN from the sail."

"Ten-four," Cowly answered. "Do you want the bridge detail topside?"

"Roger that," Boxer said. "Might as well keep the drill."

"Might as well," Cowly responded.

Within two minutes the hatch was thrown open and the first man of the deck detail clambered onto the bridge.

The RO keyed Boxer. "Skipper, all radars are operational."

"Roger that," Boxer answered; then he keyed the COMMO. "Raise the *Sea Dragon* and tell your counterpart I want to speak to Admiral Borodine."

"Aye, aye, Skipper," the COMMO said.

Boxer ran operational checks from the COMCOMP on the bridge and was satisfied that he still had full operational capability.

The COMMO keyed Boxer. "Admiral Borodine is ready to speak to you."

"Patch him through," Boxer said.

"Aye, aye, Skipper," the COMMO answered.

"Igor," Boxer said, "I want to deliver your men to you."

"Good."

"But there's a slight problem. Your people don't seem to understand this is a private matter. I can't give you a rendezvous point unless I know exactly where your attack submarines and surface ships are located. You have my word I will not attack them, unless they attack me. But I must know where they are."

Borodine was silent.

"Unless you can come up with another way for me to protect my ship, then I ask you to agree to mine," Boxer said.

"I must confer with my people," Borodine responded.

"Understood."

"I will contact you as soon as I have an answer," Borodine said.

Boxer switched off the mike. By asking for the position of the Russian ships, he was letting their captains know he intended to destroy them if they made any hostile move against the *Barracuda.*

The COMMO keyed Boxer. "Skipper, a priority one-zero from headquarters."

"Patch it through," Boxer said. He had expected Mason or Tysin to radio.

"Tysin here," Tysin announced.

"Mason here," Mason said.

Boxer grinned. Where one was the other was sure to be. "Boxer here," he told them.

"I thought the matter of the Russian prisoners was settled," Tysin said.

"It was," Boxer responded. "I will return them to the *Sea Dragon*. It takes some time to make the necessary arrangements."

"You're not going to believe what the Russians tell you, are you?"

"No. But I will believe whatever Admiral Borodine tells me."

"Your orders are to transport those Russian prisoners to our base in the Seychelles," Mason said.

"With all due respect, Admiral, you must be misinformed. I do not have any prisoners, Russian or any other, aboard the *Barracuda*. I do have guests, who are here at my invitation."

"This time," Tysin said angrily, "you won't get away with it. This time I'll have your hide: I'll break you."

"Out," Boxer answered, switching off his mike. "So much," he said under his breath, "for friendly relations." But from the moment he had met Henry Tysin, he had no illusions about the kind of chief he was going to be. And as for Mason, he was a horse's ass when he knew him at Annapolis and he was still a horse's ass, even though he was the Chief of Naval Operations. The rank and the title didn't change the man. It only made him more dangerous...

# CHAPTER 2

Borodine paced the deck, glancing now and then at the COMCOMP. He was a solidly built, fair complexioned man with blond hair, which was turning gray, a bearded strong jaw and a bull neck. "How can I give Boxer the positions of our ships, when I don't even know them?" he said aloud.

"You can tell him that," Viktor Korzenko, his EXO answered. "He might believe you."

"In his place would you believe me?"

"That would depend —"

The COMMO keyed Borodine. "Admiral Polyakov is ready to speak to you."

Borodine sat down at the COMCOMP. "Roger that… Connect him," he said.

"Aye, aye, Comrade Admiral," the COMMO answered.

A moment later Polyakov was on the air. "I have transferred my command to the *Moskva*," he said. "The *Minsk* and *Kiev* will be able to be sufficiently repaired for their homeward voyage at our base in the Republic of Malagasy."

"Very good," Borodine responded.

"The damage, though extensive, was not nearly as extensive as the DCO had first reported."

"First reports are sometimes misleading," Borodine said, wondering who the DCO was. Polyakov would probably have the man's balls hung on the jackstaff.

"I have already contacted Moscow and explained the causes and nature of our failure to secure and hold the beach."

*I bet you did*, Borodine said to himself, but made no comment to Polyakov, who had been given overall command of the mission because he's the Premier's future son-in-law.

"Moscow wants to salvage something from the disaster," Polyakov continued.

Borodine felt a tightening sensation in his gut even before Polyakov said, "We will destroy the *Barracuda*."

"My assault team is still —"

"Moscow understands that," replied Polyakov.

"I'm fucking glad they understand it," Borodine exploded, "because I don't. Comrade Admiral Boxer was willing to return—"

"The matter is closed," Polyakov said.

"I will speak to Comrade Admiral Gorshkov about this."

"That you may do," Polyakov answered smoothly. "But it will do you no good. The matter has already been decided."

Borodine said nothing. The man's political influence far outweighed the lives of the hundred men in the assault team.

"Moscow wants results," Polyakov said.

Borodine remained silent.

"If we are lucky, your Comrade Admiral Boxer will be forced to the surface and — well, I'm sure he'll surrender rather than risk the destruction of his ship and the loss of his men."

Borodine uttered a harsh bark of laughter. "Comrade Admiral," he said, "with all due respect, you're a fool if that's what you really think will happen. Let me remind you, Comrade Admiral Boxer has already damaged two of our carriers, sank an attack submarine and —"

"I know what he has done," Polyakov responded, cutting Borodine off, "which is why he must be stopped."

"I will not lure him into a trap," Borodine said.

"Comrade Admiral Gorshkov was sure you'd say that and to tell the truth, so was I," Polyakov said. "But you won't have to do anything other than tell him you cannot give him a rendezvous point and what he does with the troops, Moscow says, is no longer any concern of yours. Knowing your Comrade Admiral, he will not take them to any American base, where he knows they will be interned and his government will play politics with them. He will do the next best thing to rendezvousing with you: he will find one of our fishing trawlers and turn your men over to the ship's captain."

"And we just happen to have a fishing trawler nearby," Borodine said sarcastically, since all fishing vessels were part of the Soviet Navy.

"The *Boris Tsindelis*," Polyakov answered. "She has already taken up a position five hundred miles due south of your position. Comrade Boxer will get a fix on her from an American satellite. And when he comes close to our fishing trawler, you and the other two attack boats will go into action; as soon as that happens you will radio me and *Moskva* and the *Leningrad* will join the attack."

After a few moments' consideration, Borodine said, "It might work."

"It will," Polyakov laughed. "The trick is to get Comrade Boxer where we want him. The captain of the *Tsindelis* will use his radio just enough to allow Comrade Boxer to ID her, that and the information he gets from the satellite, should do it."

"It should," Borodine grudgingly admitted. "But I have to warn you, Comrade Boxer has a strange turn of mind. Be prepared for the unexpected."

"You seem to think he has supernatural powers," Polyakov commented.

There was an obvious sneer in his voice to which Borodine refused to respond.

"Your Comrade Captain Boxer will not get away this time. The trap is baited."

"With the lives of my men," Borodine said sourly.

"Just consider it lucky that he has already taken one-third of the bait," Polyakov replied. "And as for the other two-thirds, you will feed him one-third and when he discovers that the *Boris Tsindelis* is less than ten hours away, he'll head for her and we'll be there to close the trap."

Borodine ran his hand over his beard. "What specifically do you want me to tell —"

"Tell him that you cannot give him the coordinates of any of the vessels under my command. Tell him that Moscow will not permit it. Tell him that he is free to deliver the Russian troops he has on board to any Russian port, base or commercial type ship. Make sure he understands that the matter is out of your hands."

"Roger that," Borodine answered and switching off the radio, he turned to Viktor. "Polyakov has brought Moscow into the situation. We will not retrieve our men. Instead, we will use them as bait to destroy the *Barracuda*."

Viktor emitted a low whistle; then asked, "Do you think it will work?"

"Polyakov thinks that if we can sufficiently damage the *Barracuda*, she'll be forced to fight on the surface and if she does, Comrade Admiral Boxer will surrender, or risk losing his ship and crew."

"And our assault force," Viktor said.

Borodine nodded and explained Polyakov's plan.

"It might work," Viktor agreed.

"It might," Borodine answered and keying the COMMO, he told him to raise the *Barracuda*.

The *Barracuda was* down fifty feet and making twenty knots.

Boxer switched off the mike and for several moments stared at the COMCOMP without being aware of what the instruments were reading; then he turned to Cowly. "We can't return Igor's men. Moscow won't let him give us the positions of any of the surface craft, or subs."

"What the hell are we going to do with them?"

Boxer stood up and began to pace back and forth in the narrow confines of the bridge. Finally, he stopped and said, "I'm sure as hell not going to turn those men over to some base commander and let Dawson become a hero."

"And we sure as hell can't deliver them to a Russian base," Cowly responded.

"Igor said we could put them aboard any Russian commercial vessel we might encounter," Boxer commented.

"There are damn few of them in this part of the world."

Boxer agreed and added, "But before I do anything else, I'm going to tell Major Khmyz the latest development. I want to reassure him and his men that we will find a way of repatriating them and that delay has been caused by their government and has nothing to do with me. I don't want a replay of what happened when we had Borodine's crew on board the *Shark*. I don't want the major, or any of his men, to start thinking about taking over the *Barracuda*."

"Do you think he'll believe you?" Cowly asked.

"I sure as hell hope so," Boxer answered and he keyed the ship's security officer. "Escort Major Khmyz to the bridge," he said.

"Aye, aye, Skipper," the security officer answered.

Boxer returned to the COMCOMP. "Sail down," he said.

"Sail going down," Cowly responded. "All systems green."

"Roger that," Boxer said. He keyed the DO. "Make one-hundred feet."

"Making one-hundred feet," the DO answered.

Boxer watched the instruments on the COMCOMP and every few moments glanced up at the depth gauge. "Looking good," he commented aloud. The *Barracuda* still had to complete her sea trials. Boxer expected to do that on the way back to the States.

The security officer, with Major Khmyz in tow, requested permission to come on the bridge and speak to the captain.

"Permission granted," Cowly answered.

Boxer faced the security officer and Major Khmyz. "I hope you and your men are comfortable. As comfortable as the situation allows?"

Khmyz nodded.

"Have your men eaten?" Boxer asked.

Khmyz smiled. "Using chopsticks was strange to them and members of your crew had to give them a few lessons. But they soon caught on."

Boxer laughed. "The same thing happens when we have a new man assigned," he said. "Everyone in the United States does not know how to eat with chopsticks." He was having difficulty finding the right words to explain the situation to the major.

"Comrade Admiral," Khmyz said, "I have the feeling that you had me brought here to tell me something and not to engage in small talk."

Boxer nodded. He not only admired the man's insight, he also appreciated the man's frankness. "An unforeseen problem has developed with regard to returning you and your men to the *Sea Dragon*."

Khmyz nodded but said nothing.

The DO keyed Boxer. "One-hundred feet, Skipper, and level."

"Roger that," Boxer said and checked the DDRO against the depth gauge: the reading on the two instruments matched; then he faced the major and explained the situation.

"Moscow, eh," Khmyz responded; then quickly added, "You can bet that Comrade Admiral Polyakov had something to do with that."

"Do you think it would help if I raised him on the radio and—"

Khmyz shook his head. "He is not the kind of man you can reason with about anything."

Boxer pursed his lips and then he said, "I will find a way of returning you and your men. But you will have to trust me."

"Neither I, or my men will find that difficult to do," Khmyz answered. "Besides, I can keep what you told me to myself for as long as I wish. I do not have to share it with anyone in my command."

Boxer shook the man's hand. "I will let you know if there's any change as soon as I know."

"With all due respect, Comrade Admiral," Khmyz said, "I would not waste my time speaking to Comrade Admiral Polyakov. I'd find another way."

"I intend to do that," Boxer answered and shifting his eyes to the security officer, he said, "Please escort the major back to the mess area."

"Aye, aye, Skipper," the man said.

Boxer waited until the security officer and Khmyz were well out of earshot before he looked toward Cowly and said, "Unless I make some powerful magic, I sure as hell don't know how I'm going to get him and his men back in Russian hands."

"There must be some Russian ships in the area," Cowly said. "What about tankers? We could lie off the Red Sea and —"

Suddenly Boxer snapped his fingers. He keyed the CIC. "How long ago did you tap into our Sea Scan satellite?" he asked.

"Just before we dove," the officer answered.

"What do we have in the way of Russian ships in this sector of the Indian Ocean?" Boxer answered.

"The cruisers *Moskva* and *Leningrad* are —"

"Commercial type vessels… Any tankers?"

"None… But there's a large fish factory … the *Boris Tsindelis*. She has moved within five hundred miles of us within the last few hours."

"Is she large enough to take the Russians off our hands?"

"Yes."

"Give me the last known position," Boxer said.

"One-two north, five-two east," the officer responded.

"Roger that," Boxer said and keying the COMMO, he asked, "Are you getting any signals from one-two north latitude, fifty-two east longitude?"

"The usual. It's a Russian fishing factory."

"How do you know that?" Boxer asked. He was sure the COMMO did not understand Russian.

"Now and then its COMMO has ID'd the ship in English. I've been listening to it since we've come into this area."

"What area?"

"Skipper, the area we're in now."

"You mean since we went into action?"

"Before that, Skipper. The *Boris Tsindelis* was a thousand miles south of where she was only a few days ago. And in the last few hours I don't think she's done much fishing."

"Why?"

"She's been moving too fast. Probably at one-five knots or better."

"For how many hours?" Boxer asked.

"Ten, maybe twelve."

"Roger that," Boxer answered, "and thanks."

"Ten-four, skipper," the COMMO said.

Boxer leaned back into his command chair; then facing Cowly, he said, "I had almost taken the bait."

Cowly raised his eyebrows.

"The *Boris Tsindelis* was the bait," Boxer said. "That's where the attack subs will be waiting for us. Polyakov had moved that ship close enough for me to think I could put Igor's assault team aboard."

"But how could you know that?"

Boxer told him what he'd learned from the COMMO. "Put it all together and it spells trap."

"Christ, we could have been caught on the surface!" Cowly exclaimed.

Boxer rubbed his beard. "I think I'll bait a trap of my own," he said. "We'll do exactly what Polyakov wants us to do. We'll head for the *Boris Tsindelis*, only instead of being caught with our pants down, we'll be ready and waiting for them."

"But the *Sea Dragon* will be there too and you can bet the *Moskva* and the *Leningrad* will be on the surface, just out of range of our sonar."

"So will the *Sea Dragon* and the other two or three attack subs," Boxer said.

"That still gives them the odds."

Boxer shook his head. "It evens them," he said. "How clear is the water here?"

"Very clear."

"From the air do you think a pilot could see down into it about a hundred feet?"

Cowly nodded.

"Okay. We'll run at seven-five feet. Our two whirlybirds will be out scouting for us beyond the range of our sonar and our two mini-subs will be launched as soon as we know where the Russian ships are located."

"What about the *Moskva* and *Leningrad*?"

"They'll keep their distance until Polyakov is sure we can't do them any harm."

"We certainly will have the element of surprise on our side," Cowly said.

Boxer grinned and turning back to the COMCOMP, he switched on the MC. "NAVSYS and PROPULSIONSYS are going to AUTO CONTROL." Then he dialed in the last known position of the *Boris Tsindelis* into the AUTONAVSYS and dialed in a speed of two-five knots into the AUTO SPEED CONTROL. "Now," he said, "all we have to do is get ready and wait."

"Skipper," Cowly said, "*Moskva*, the *Leningrad* and the *Boris Tsindelis* have surface to air radar. If they spot our whirlybirds, someone might tumble to the fact that we're onto them."

"The pilots will have to ride a rollercoaster. They won't be able to hold the same altitude for more than two or three minutes. But most of the time, they'll have to fly at about fifty feet off the deck."

"Are you going to tell the major?"

"Negative," Boxer answered and looking at the NAVCLOCK, he said, "We have one-zero hours before we reach the *Tsindelis*. During that time I want every man to have rested and eaten."

"Aye, aye, Skipper."

"For the time being we'll keep our present depth and operating status."

"So far everything looks good," Cowly commented.

With a nod, Boxer agreed; then he said, "Take the CONN. I'm going to get something to eat; then I'm going to my quarters."

Cowly stepped up to the COMCOMP.

"If we play this right," Boxer said, moving off the command chair, "we should be able to give the Russians one hell of a surprise."

"I was thinking exactly the same thing," Cowly answered.

Before he left the bridge, Boxer took one last look at the COMCOMP: all the instrument readings were normal.


Borodine drank coffee and munched at a piece of bobka at a table in the mess area. He was formulating his battle plans. He would deploy the three attack subs at each of the apexes of an equilateral triangle in the center of which would be the *Boris Tsindelis*. Two of the subs would always be twenty-five nautical miles from the computer-calculated approach of the *Barracuda*. His own ship would shadow the *Barracuda* along its projected course line and choosing the time and place, he would coordinate the attack. The *Moskva* and the *Leningrad* would remain over the horizon, some thirty nautical miles to the south of the *Tsindelis* and would only join in the attack if the *Barracuda* was forced to fight on the surface. There were two variables that bothered him: the first was the course projected by the computer for the *Barracuda*. If the real course varied too much to the left or the right of the projected one, then Boxer would be able to pick up the *Sea Dragon* and one of the other boats on his sonar. But what bothered him even more was Boxer's unique twist of mind and that was something for which he could never account, regardless of what information he would feed into the COMCOMP.

Boxer lay in his bunk and thought about Francine, the woman whom he was going to marry when he returned. She had literally taken him off the street when he was at his worst, when the claustrophobia was so bad he had lost all sense of where he was and what he was doing. He had run until he had exhausted himself and when that had happened, he had found himself facing her. Now, whenever an attack came, he evoked her face again and found the strength to gain control of himself.

Boxer realized that Francine wouldn't want him to do what he was going to do. She'd want him to change course and find some other Russian ship, or bring Igor's men back to the States and let the government return them. "But I can't do that," he whispered. "I can't turn tail and run. I didn't want this fight. I wanted to return a hundred or so brave men to their ship, to their commander. But that's not the way it's going to be." He pursed his lips; then he said, "With luck, I should be home in ten days, twenty at the most and then —"

The COMMO keyed him. "Skipper, a priority seven message from headquarters."

"Read it."

"Return to home base immediately."

"Send the following message… Use a priority nine. Message acknowledged. Will change course after engaging Russian force."

The COMMO reread the message.

"That's it," Boxer said. "Send it."

'Aye, aye, Skipper," the COMMO answered.

Boxer sat in front of the COMCOMP. He switched on the MC. "All hands now hear this… All hands now hear this… As of now, we are on combat status… That means battle stations for everyone … security officer… Place two machine guns at the entrance to the mess area… Major Khmyz, your men will not be harmed if they remain within the mess area… Moscow has made it impossible for me to return you to your ship at this time… All hands, we will be going into action very soon… Good luck!"

"Those machine guns are not going to make our Russian guests happy," Cowly commented.

"They're there to make me happy," Boxer answered.

The SO keyed Boxer. "Surface target, nine-five degrees… Range twenty-five thousand yards… Speed one-five knots… Course zero-five degrees… ID the *Boris Tsindelis*."

"Roger that," Boxer answered and keyed the EO. "Reduce speed to one-zero knots."

"Reducing speed to one-zero knots," the EO said.

Boxer looked over his shoulder at Cowly. "When we come within twelve thousand yards, we'll launch our mini-subs and at five thousand yards we'll launch our whirlybirds."

"Sub operators and pilots have been thoroughly briefed," Cowly answered.

Boxer nodded and turned back to the COMCOMP, where a three-dimensional image of the *Tsindelis* was on the sonar scope. He was sure she didn't have the *Barracuda* on her sonar yet and putting himself in Igor's place, he would have the COMCOMP plot a projected course for the *Barracuda*; then he would shadow her, just out of sonar range. He looked at the image of the *Tsindelis* again. "If I were Igor," he said to Cowly, "I'd put two of the three boats somewhere on a base line north of the *Tsindelis* and use the third as back-up for any of the other two, or to the south, just in case we might decide to come in from that direction."

The SO reported a new range for the *Tsindelis*… She was now twenty-thousand yards away.

Boxer keyed the SO. "Go to one-zero knots," he said.

"Reducing speed to one-zero knots," the SO answered.

Boxer keyed the launch bay. "Prepare to launch the Guppy One and Guppy Two."

"Aye, aye, Skipper," the launch bay officer answered.

Boxer activated the launch bay video. Both mini-subs were in their cradles. Each mini-sub had a crew of three: a pilot, who was in command, a fire control officer and engineering officer, who controlled all the sub's operating systems.

Boxer keyed the DO. "Make seven-five feet," he said.

"Making seven-five feet."

Boxer looked at the *Tsindelis* again. She was eighteen-thousand yards away. Boxer guessed that her sonar would probably pick them up when the distance between them had narrowed to something between fifteen and ten thousand yards and that from that moment on, she would vector each of them to the target. He keyed the crews of the mini-subs. "Once you're launched," Boxer said, "stay close to us. I don't want you to give the Russians separate sonar images. I'll tell you when to break and attack. Remember you might encounter Guppies from the *Sea Dragon*. Destroy them. They're your first target."

"Aye, aye, Skipper," both pilots answered almost in unison.

"After you get the Guppies go for the attack subs."

"Affirmative, Skipper," one of the pilots said, while the other responded with the customary, "Aye, aye, Skipper."

Boxer said to Cowly, "Give me time to target range of fifteen thousand yards."

"Aye, aye, Skipper," Cowly answered.

Boxer keyed the helicopter launch officer. "Prepare to launch," he said.

"Pilots in place… Birds ready," the launch officer reported.

"Roger that," Boxer responded.

"Skipper," Cowly said, "target range of fifteen thousand yards in zero-six minutes and two-two seconds."

Boxer nodded and keyed the launch bay officer. "Launch Guppies in zero-six minutes."

"Aye, aye, Skipper," the launch bay officer said.

Boxer keyed the EO. "Activate ECM system."

"ECM system activated," the EO replied.

The SO keyed Boxer. "Skipper, I caught something at two-six-five degrees; then it vanished. I couldn't get a range on it."

"Roger that," Boxer said and glancing at Cowly, he reported what the SO had just told him. Then he added, "I'm going to take a chance. Order a firing mission from CIC. I want them to calculate a target at two-six-five degrees at a range of twenty-five to twenty-eight thousand yards. Feed the info into a sonar homing torpedo and control the firing sequence from the CIC."

"Aye, aye, Skipper."

Suddenly the pinging of the *Tsindelis'* sonar sounded through the *Barracuda*.

Boxer switched on the MC. "They know we're here. But we've got a few surprises for them."

The SO keyed Boxer. "Target eight-four degrees... Range fifteen-thousand yards... Speed one-five knots... On course of zero-five degrees."

"Roger that," Boxer answered.

A red light began to flash, indicating that the launch bay doors were open and the Guppies were moving out.

Boxer looked at the video and that's exactly what he saw. He keyed the helicopter launch officer. "Going to launch depth... Stand by to launch Red Birds One and Two at five-zero feet."

"Aye, aye, Skipper."

Boxer keyed the DO. "Make five-zero feet."

"Making five-zero feet," the DO answered.

Another red light started to flash.

"Torpedo away," Cowly reported.

"Roger that," Boxer answered, watching the DDRO.

As soon as the *Barracuda* reached fifty feet, a third red light flashed.

The helicopter launch officer keyed Boxer. "Red Birds away," he said.

"Roger that," Boxer answered and he keyed the forward torpedo room officer. "Arm and load torpedo one... Firing data slaved from sonar."

"Arming and loading torpedo one," the TO answered.

Boxer keyed the CIC. "What's the sonar feedback?"

"Target found... On course... Zero-two minutes to impact."

"Any target evasive action?"

"No indication of any."

"Roger that," Boxer answered.

"Skipper," Cowly said, "both birds are in the air... Holding at one-zero feet above deck."

"Roger that," Boxer said.

The forward TO keyed Boxer. "Torpedo ready... Target data slaved from sonar... Will continue to feed."

"Stand by to fire," Boxer answered.

"Standing by," FTO said.

Suddenly a low thunder-like explosion rumbled through the water.

Boxer checked the Time To Target Clock. Two minutes and thirty-five seconds had elapsed between the time the torpedo was launched and the explosion. "That's no proof we hit anything," Boxer said.

"I'd settle for just enough damage to take it out of action," Cowly responded.

"Repeat the same firing mission," Boxer said, "but this time use nine-zero degrees."

"Aye, aye, Skipper," Cowly answered.

Boxer keyed the FTO. "Fire one."

"One fired," the FTO said.

Boxer watched the TTC.

The COMMO keyed Boxer. "Skipper, very heavy traffic between the Russians."

"Roger that," Boxer responded; then to Cowly he said, "The COMMO says there's heavy radio traffic between the Russians."

"That could mean we did damage or sank the sub."

The TTC stopped and another explosion rumbled over the *Barracuda*.

Boxer checked the scope. The *Tsindelis* was listing to her star'b'd side.

The SO keyed Boxer. "Multiple targets nine-zero degrees... Range twenty-two thousand yards... Speed four-zero knots... Depth... two-five-zero, closing fast."

"Mag-plats?" Boxer questioned.

"Looks like the real thing," the SO answered.

Boxer studied the images on the scope. There were four of them. Suddenly a fifth image resolved itself on the screen. Boxer keyed Guppy One. "Vector nine-zero degrees," he said. "Ignore the first four targets go for the fifth... Range twenty-thousand yards."

"Ten-four."

"Make your attack from above," Boxer said.

"Aye, aye, Skipper," the pilot answered.

Boxer keyed Red Bird One. "Hit the *Tsindelis*... Go for her antennae."

"Ten-four, Skipper," the pilot answered.

"Red Bird Two," Boxer said. "Go up to one-thousand feet... Make a recon sweep of three-six-zero degrees, on a radius of zero-five miles."

"Aye, aye, Skipper," Red Bird Two answered.

Boxer checked the TTC. The second hand touched zero.

CIC keyed Boxer. "Torpedo still moving. No target on the screen."

"Destroy," Boxer said.

A moment later a thunder-like sound swept over the *Barracuda*.

The SO keyed Boxer. Target six-five degrees... Range twenty-four thousand five-hundred yards... Speed four-zero degrees... Depth two-five-zero feet... Course three-one-zero degrees... ID the *Sea Dragon*."

"Roger that," Boxer answered.

Boxer keyed the EO. "Flank speed," he ordered.

"Going to flank speed," the EO said.

The SO keyed Boxer. "Target nine-five degrees... Speed three-five knots... Depth one-five feet... Course two-zero degrees... ID type Victor Two Class."

"Roger that," Boxer answered. He glanced at the helmsman. "Mahony, come to one-seven-zero degrees."

"Coming to one-seven-degrees," Mahony said.

Red Bird Two keyed Boxer. "Base one, the *Tsindelis* is dead in the water and burning aft… Red Bird One going in on the deck… Nothing else."

"Extend your recon radius by five-thousand yards," Boxer said.

"Ten-four."

Boxer turned to the sonar display… Guppy One was closing on the Russian mini-sub… The Mag-plats were off the screen… Boxer keyed Guppy Two. "Vector five-nine degrees… Use killer darts at maximum range."

"Ten-four, Skipper," the pilot answered.

Red Bird One keyed Boxer. "Antennae out… Antennae out… Going to five —"

"Red Bird One," Boxer said. "Say again… Say again…"

"Base One, this is Red Bird Two… Red Bird One is down… Red Bird One is down."

"Roger that," Boxer answered.

The SO keyed Boxer. "All targets holding course," he reported.

"Roger that," Boxer said. "Start calling out range at fifteen thousand yards."

"Aye, aye, Skipper," the SO replied.

Boxer keyed the CIC. "Start Combat Operational Computer when *Sea Dragon* comes within fifteen-thousand yards… I want a continuous readout of operational and firing sequences… I'll slave them in on my CIC scope."

"Aye, aye, Skipper," the CIC section officer said.

"Guppy One to Base," the pilot called, "Guppy One to base."

"Base copying," Boxer said.

"Eight-thousand yards out… Target ahead… Salvoing killer darts."

"Roger that," Boxer answered, switching on the UWIS. For a moment the picture was scrambled.

An explosion rolled through the water.

The picture suddenly cleared. Boxer watched pieces of debris float downward. He keyed Guppy One. "Guppy One and Red Bird One are down," he said. Cowly didn't answer.

Boxer keyed the MO. "Arm and load ASROC's One, Two and Three."

"Aye, aye, Skipper," the MO said.

"Target bearing nine-eight degrees… Range seven-thousand yards… Speed four-five knots… Depth two-hundred feet… Closing fast."

Boxer checked the scope. The Russian mini-sub was heading straight for them.

"Base one, this is Red Bird Two… Spotted sub, bearing four-two degrees from your position… Estimate depth one-five feet… Speed less than four-zero knots… Trailing oil."

"Attack," Boxer ordered. "Attack."

"Ten-four, Skipper," the pilot answered.

Boxer keyed Guppy Two and relayed the information from Red Bird Two. "Coordinate attack with Red Bird Two."

"Aye, aye, Skipper," the pilot said.

Boxer checked the UWIS. Beyond the mini-sub the *Sea Dragon* was clearly visible. He keyed the FCO. "Stand by to fire killer darts."

"Aye, aye, Skipper."

Boxer flicked a switch. "Azimuth, range and speed of target being fed into FCCOMP."

"FC data into killer darts," the FCO reported.

"Switching FC to COMCOMP," Boxer said, checking the mini-sub's position on the UWIS and then the sonar scope. The target was five hundred yards closed. "Firing killer darts," he said, pressing the red FC button.

The killer darts were blurs on the UWIS and sonar screens. But ten seconds after they were fired Boxer saw the Russian Guppy disintegrate on the UWIS and the blips vanish from the sonar. Moments later the sound of the explosion reached the *Barracuda*.

The SO keyed Boxer. "Target one-four-five degrees... Range seven hundred yards... Speed five-zero knots... Depth three hundred feet... ID ASROC."

"Roger that" Boxer answered calmly. "Helmsman, come to course two-five degrees."

"Coming to course two-five degrees," Mahony answered.

Boxer checked the fathometer. Between the *Barracuda* and the bottom was six hundred feet. He hit the klaxon three times, switched on the MC and said, "Crash dive... Crash dive." A moment later he keyed the DO, "Come level at four hundred feet."

"Level at four hundred feet," the DO answered.

Boxer watched the sonar. The ASROC made a complete circle above them.

The SO keyed Boxer. "The *Sea Dragon* at fifteen thousand yards... Heading, course and depth the same."

"Roger that," Boxer answered. He knew the *Sea Dragon*'s depth would change to match his. He keyed the MO. "Cancel fire mission."

"Missile fire mission cancelled," the MO replied.

The SO keyed Boxer. "*Sea Dragon* diving."

"Roger that," Boxer said and keyed the FTO. "Arm and load tubes three and four with base guided torpedoes… Maximum range of ten thousand yards."

"Aye, aye, Skipper," the FTO answered.

Red Bird Two keyed Boxer. "Coordinating attack with Guppy Two… Going in now!"

Boxer acknowledged the message.

The FTO keyed Boxer. "Tubes three and four ready."

"Roger that," Boxer answered. "Stand by to fire."

"Stand by," the FTO responded.

Boxer watched the *Sea Dragon* dive on the UWIS. He was waiting until the *Sea Dragon* reached six hundred feet before he gave the order to fire the torpedoes…

Borodine's eyes were riveted to the UWIS. He had warned Polyakov that Boxer had a "strange twist of mind" and because of it one Guppy was lost, one sub was badly damaged and under further attack; and the *Tsindelis* was on fire.

The COMMO keyed Borodine. "Attack ship *Delta* requests permission to break off the attack."

"Patch me through to her captain," Borodine said.

"Aye, aye, Comrade Admiral," the COMMO answered.

Within moments Borodine was in direct communication with the captain of the *Delta*.

"We are taking fire from a Guppy and a helicopter," the captain explained. "I have a damaged forward ballast tank. My electronic steering control is out and I have a partially flooded aft torpedo room."

"Roger that," Borodine answered. "Can you survive?"

"Only if I withdraw."

Suddenly a red light began to flash on the COMCOMP in front of Borodine. "Withdraw and good luck," he told the captain.

The DCO keyed Borodine. "We have an electrical fire in the aft torpedo room."

"Can you get to it quickly?"

Even before the DCO answered the smoke alarm went off.

Borodine cursed.

"Aft torpedo room must be evacuated and all blower systems shut down," the DCO said.

"Roger that," Borodine answered and turning to Viktor, he said, "Pull the men out of the aft torpedo room and shut down all the blower systems." Borodine turned his attention back to the COMCOMP. They had reached a depth of five-hundred-fifty feet. He had to decide whether he was going to complete the dive to six hundred feet, or whether he'd abort and break off the attack. He keyed the DCO. "Can you get to that fire?"

"Not without taking up some of the deck plates," the DCO answered.

Borodine looked at the gauges indicating the quality of the ship's air... It was rapidly deteriorating. The carbon dioxide level was almost in the red zone. He made his decision! "Helmsman," he barked, "come to course one-eight-zero."

"Coming to course one-eight-zero," the helmsman answered.

Borodine keyed the DO. "Going to emergency surface," he said.

"Going to emergency surface," the DO repeated.

Borodine watched the COMCOMP. Diving planes were set at their maximum lift angle... All ballast was blown... He looked at the carbon dioxide level: it stayed just below the red.

The SO keyed Boxer. "Target bearing nine-zero degrees... Range fifteen-thousand yards and increasing... Depth four-hundred feet and going up... Course nine-zero degrees... ID the *Sea Dragon*."

"Roger that," Boxer answered, watching the *Sea Dragon* on the UWIS. "Looks like she's breaking off the action," he commented and motioned to Cowly to join him at the COMCOMP.

"Maybe Igor thinks we'll follow him?" Cowly suggested.

Guppy Two keyed Boxer. "Target on new course... Trailing oil... Red Bird Two scored one direct hit... Low on fuel... Will have to ditch in zero-five minutes... Can pick up birdman, or press attack."

"Pick up pilot and return to base," Boxer answered.

"Ten-four, Skipper," the pilot answered.

Boxer rubbed his beard. "Igor has problems, or he wouldn't be heading for the surface." He keyed the COMMO. "Are the Russians talking up a storm?"

"Negative, Skipper... They've been quieter than usual."

"Ten-four," Boxer answered.

"He's at three-hundred and fifty feet and still going up," Cowly said.

"Emergency surfacing?"

"Looks like it."

Boxer's eyes went to the FC indicators. There were two torpedoes loaded and armed. If he gave the order to fire them within the next few minutes, he could probably destroy the *Sea Dragon*, or at the very least cause heavy damage. He keyed the FTO. "Hold firing mission," he said.

"Holding firing mission," the FTO answered.

The COMMO keyed Boxer. "Skipper, lots of Russian communications now."

"Roger that," Boxer responded.

"Christ, will you look at that!" Cowly exclaimed.

The *Sea Dragon* lurched to one side.

"An onboard explosion," Boxer said.

"Looks like that," Cowly replied. "But she's still heading for the surface… She's leaking oil."

Boxer turned to Mahony. "Come to zero-nine degrees," he said; then switched on the MC. "Now hear this… All hands now hear this… switching to AUTOCONTROL… Switching to AUTOCONTROL." Then to Cowly, he said, "We're going to the surface."

Cowly nodded.

Boxer began to adjust the controls on the AUTODIV section of the COMCOMP. "We'll surface slowly." Then he added, "Igor would do the same for me if the situation were reversed."

"That's something we have to believe," Cowly said.

"That's something I do believe," Boxer answered. "If I didn't—"

"Skipper, I believe it too." And pointing to the UWIS, he said, "She's going even slower than before."

"Probably taking water," Boxer answered.

The SO keyed Boxer. "Skipper, Guppy One at one-two degrees… Range one-thousand yards and holding."

"Roger that," Boxer answered. He was so intent on watching the *Sea Dragon* on the UWIS that he hadn't checked the sonar scope for several minutes. He keyed the COMM. "Contact Guppy One and have it follow us to the surface."

"Aye, aye, Skipper," the COMMO answered.

Suddenly the infra-red sensor warning light began to flash.

"That heat is coming from the *Sea Dragon*," Cowly said. "They must have a fire aboard, or their reactor has gone critical."

Boxer looked at the radiation levels. "Fire," he said and rubbing his beard, he quickly played out several scenarios in his mind. One of them had the other Russian vessels converging on the *Sea Dragon* and *Barracuda* and finding himself enveloped by overwhelming fire power. And another in which he placed himself inside the *Sea Dragon* and because he had been in a similar situation, he knew what was happening. "They'll be lucky if they reach the surface alive," he said to Cowly.

Again Boxer rubbed his beard. "Okay, Polyakov, I have a surprise for you." And keying the COMMO, he said, "Open a channel for me."

"Aye, aye, Skipper," the COMMO answered and a few moments later, he added, "Channel opened."

"Comrade Admiral Polyakov, this is Admiral Jack Boxer, captain of the American submarine *Barracuda*... I am following your ship, the *Sea Dragon*, to the surface to render whatever assistance I can... She has some sort of fire aboard and has suffered an explosion. I know you are either listening to this transmission, or it is being recorded by your communications officer. I am warning you that I will fire on any Russian vessel or submarine that comes within our firing range, which as you probably know by now, covers a considerable distance with deadly accuracy. Do not attempt to come close. Comrade Admiral Borodine or I will advise you of the situation."

"That should turn him purple," Cowly commented.

"More like red," Boxer answered with a straight face. "But definitely purple for Mason and Tysin."

The COMMO keyed Boxer. "Comrade Admiral Polyakov is on the open channel."

"Patch him through," Boxer said.

"Aye, aye, Skipper," the COMMO responded.

"Comrade Admiral Boxer," Polyakov said stiffly. "You are interfering with a Russian naval exercise and it is my duty to inform you that a formal complaint will be lodged with your government."

"That's not my concern," Boxer answered. "You do what you must do and I will do what I must do. Keep your ships out of range. Do not make the mistake of thinking I am bluffing. I am not."

There was a long pause before Polyakov said, "You leave me no choice. My ships will remain out of range."

Bleary-eyed and sweating profusely, Borodine keyed the COMMO. "A channel to Comrade Admiral Boxer."

"Aye, aye, Comrade Admiral," the COMMO answered.

Borodine had heard the conversation between Boxer and Polyakov and marveled at Boxer's courage. The man didn't seem to be afraid of anyone or anything.

"Channel opened," the COMMO reported.

"Jack, I have a runaway ship," Borodine said without any preliminary conversation. "My men are too weak to open the hatches. Most are close to unconsciousness."

"Explain," Boxer answered.

"Carbon dioxide level very high," Borodine said.

"Roger that," Boxer answered.

"Reading five-zero feet to surface," Borodine said.

"Five-zero feet," Boxer responded.

"Slowing to one zero knots … ship not responding… Keep four-zero knots."

"You will reach surface in zero-two minutes," Boxer said. "Have you emergency exterior unlatching mechanism for your hatches?"

"Negative. Blow aft hatch, if you can," Borodine answered. Suddenly a series of green lights began to flash on the COMCOMP. "I have a surface indication," Borodine said.

"Negative," Boxer told him. "You have two-five feet to go."

"Can't talk any more," Borodine said. "Can't talk…"

Boxer looked at Cowly. "We'll ask for volunteers from our men and the Russians to board the *Sea Dragon*."

"But how will they —"

"We'll run alongside and get as close as we can to it," Boxer said. "The men will have to jump from our deck to theirs."

Suddenly several green lights on the COMCOMP began to flash and the AUTODIV INDICATOR started to ring.

Boxer switched on the MC. "Deck detail stand by… Gun turret details stand by."

Cowly returned to his station.

"Raise sail," Boxer said.

"Sail going up," Cowly responded.

"Deck and turret details topside," Boxer ordered. Then to Cowly he said, "I want you on the bridge with me."

"Aye, aye, Skipper," Cowly responded.

"Mahony, on the bridge topside."

"Aye, aye, Skipper," Mahony said.

Boxer turned to one of the other officers on the bridge. "Take the CONN. Hold her steady as she goes."

"Aye, aye, Skipper," the man answered.

Boxer crossed the deck, swung undogged the bulkhead hatch leading to the sail and hurried up the ladder leading to the bridge. Moments later he undogged the hatch and clambered up to the bridge. He switched all control to the bridge COMCOMP and over the MC told the officer below, "I have the CONN."

"Ten-four, Skipper," officer said.

Boxer took a quick report from the deck and turret details.

The two turrets were operational and deck detail was standing by for further orders.

"I need four volunteers," he said over the MC. "Two from my crew and two from our Russian guests. Major Khmyz please translate my request and anything else I say to your men." Then he gave a brief description of the *Sea Dragon*'s condition and what must be done to save her crew.

"Skipper," Cowly said, "I request permission to go aboard the *Sea Dragon*."

Boxer realized Cowly was suggesting he go in his place.

"You have the CONN," Boxer answered. "Keep the ships as close as possible."

"Aye, aye, Skipper," Cowly answered. "And good luck."

In a matter of minutes, Boxer joined the ten volunteers from the crew and an equal number from Khmyz's men and Khmyz himself assembled on the forward part of the deck. Wicks was among the men from the *Barracuda*. "Didn't you have enough?" he asked.

"Skipper, I figured I might as well make a full day of it," Wicks answered in his slow western drawl.

Boxer nodded. "Might as well," he answered, looking over the men and deciding to use all of them. He assigned four teams of four men to blow the two forward and two aft hatches. Three men were given the task of slinging a three inch air hose between the *Barracuda* and the *Sea Dragon*. He and the major were going to go directly to the COMCOMP and try to regain control of the ship. He waited until Khmyz translated everything he had said; then he asked if any of the men had questions.

There weren't any.

Boxer keyed Cowly. "Bring her in close," he said.

"Aye, aye, Skipper," Cowly answered.

Boxer motioned the deck detail chief forward. "Get below and connect a three inch air hose to a pump. Have it ready to go between us and the *Sea Dragon*."

"Aye, aye, Skipper," the chief said.

Boxer keyed the demolitions officer. "I'm sending Wicks down for four half-pound charges of RDX... On a short fuse."

"Ten-four," the demolitions officer replied.

Boxer turned to the *Sea Dragon*. The two ships were running side by side. No more than two to three feet between them. He keyed Cowly. "Take us closer," he said.

"Closer," Cowly answered.

Boxer looked at the men. "Spread out... Make it a running jump. Go when you think you're ready... Good luck!"

The first man to run across the deck was a Russian. He jumped and managed to land on the *Sea Dragon*'s forward ballast tank.

The distance between the two ships narrowed.

Boxer looked at Khmyz.

The major nodded.

"Now," Boxer said, running across the deck. He leaped free of the *Barracuda* just as she rolled to the star'b'd. He was in the air. Moments later he came down on the *Sea Dragon*. His feet went out from under him. He slid toward the open water between the two boats. He clawed at the steel plates. But there was nothing for him to grab. He forced down a scream. The roar of the water between the boats deafened him. He felt himself roll; then suddenly he was yanked upward and found himself standing between one of his men and a Russian.

"Close call, Skipper," his man said.

"Close," Boxer agreed and looking at the Russian, he nodded; then he said, "Let's blow those hatches."

The explosives were tossed across to the deck of the *Sea Dragon* and quickly set. Four explosions went off in unison. The blown hatches were tossed aside and the men dropped down the open hatchways into the *Sea Dragon*.

Boxer and Khmyz rushed to the bridge. Borodine was still alive.

# CHAPTER 3

The *Barracuda* and *Sea Dragon* were lashed together and lay dead in the water. Boxer and Borodine stood on the forward deck of the *Sea Dragon*. Neither of them had much to say to the other as they watched the damage control crew from the *Sea Dragon* replace the two hatches that had been blown off.

Major Khmyz joined them. "Comrade Admiral," he said, saluting Borodine. "My men are ready to board the *Sea Dragon*."

Borodine returned the salute. "Have them come aboard."

"Aye, aye, Comrade Admiral," Khmyz answered; then with a broad smile, he looked at Boxer and said, "My men and I wish to thank you and your men for all you did for us. It is a pleasure to know you." And he offered his hand.

Boxer shook his hand. "It has been my pleasure to know you," he answered.

Khmyz turned and moved down the deck to where the two ships almost touched, before he crossed over to the *Barracuda*.

"We're being filmed," Borodine said, gesturing toward the bridge of the *Barracuda*.

"That's Colonel Dawson, commander of the ship's assault force," Boxer explained. During the past five hours it had taken to get the *Sea Dragon* sufficiently operational to return to port, Dawson had avoided any contact with either Borodine, his EXO and even Khmyz.

"Viktor and your Mister Cowly are going over some last-minute details. Your DCO had to rewire a portion of the blower control panel."

Boxer nodded. "He has drawn two schematics showing suggested changes that would eliminate the danger of another short and subsequent fire."

"You know," Borodine commented, "we probably had no more than a couple of minutes left when you came down the hatchway."

"Probably."

Borodine took several deep breaths. "You have no idea what a wonderful feeling it is to be able to fill your lungs with air. To be able to look up at the sea and the sky."

Boxer didn't answer. He wasn't about to tell him that he did indeed know the feeling, but for a very different reason…

"Do your people in Washington know what has been happening here?" Borodine asked.

"No," Boxer answered. "After my message to Polyakov, I have maintained radio silence."

"Comrade Admiral Polyakov, now there's a political animal!" Borodine exclaimed. "Engaged to the Premier's daughter, he is close to the sources of power. The man is probably in a rage that you're here and he can't get at you."

"So far, he hasn't tried. My SO has had a clear screen," Boxer said.

"I don't think he'll try any more," Borodine responded. "He's lost too much and my ship is in no condition to go into action again."

"My DCO tells me you can't go below one hundred feet," Boxer said.

"Hull damage from the two interned explosions," Borodine explained. "I have several badly distended plates on the port side."

Boxer acknowledged the information without commenting; then he said, "Kinkade is dead and Stark has had a stroke."

Borodine nodded. "From what little contact I had with either man, I always preferred Stark to Kinkade."

"He never got over Trish's death," Boxer admitted. "He was never the same man after she was killed."

"Maybe it was her life he couldn't deal with?" Borodine suggested.

Boxer shrugged. The two of them had been Trish's lovers and in truth, he had come to the conclusion that Borodine understood her better than he did.

"I'm married now," Borodine said.

Boxer's face broke into a big smile. He was glad to leave Trish's memory. "Congratulations!" he exclaimed, vigorously pumping Borodine's hand.

"And I'm soon to be a father," Borodine said proudly.

"That's marvelous!"

"And you, what about you?"

"I hope to marry when I return," Boxer said.

"Good… Very good. A man needs someone to love, someone to come home to."

Boxer agreed and then he said, "Perhaps, one day if our governments get together long enough to stop our missions, you'll be allowed to come to the States with your family."

"Maybe some day soon."

"I was sorry you couldn't come to pick up your medal," Boxer said.

Borodine smiled. "I'll bet you didn't make many friends when you suggested that the United States should give me a medal."

"Made some and lost some," Boxer admitted.

The two of them stopped talking and watched Khmyz lead his men across to the *Sea Dragon*.

"It's time for us to get underway," Boxer said.

"Time," Borodine answered.

The two walked toward the sail, stopped when they reached the place where the two ships almost touched, and shook hands.

"I'd have much preferred to visit you in Washington than meet you out here," Borodine said.

"Next time, before we go on a mission, we'll have to tell our bosses what we'd prefer to do, rather than accept what they tell us to do."

Borodine laughed. "Maybe you could get away with that, but I know I couldn't."

Boxer nodded sympathetically. "I don't think I could get away with it either. I might be able to bitch about a mission more than you can, but in the end I'd be given the choice of going or resigning."

"My choice would be limited to going or winding up in a Siberian Gulag. That's not much choice."

"Not much," Boxer agreed.

"You send my best to your future wife," Borodine said. "Tell her that —" He paused for a moment. "Tell her she's getting the best there is."

"Tell your wife I look forward to meeting her," Boxer said and he crossed over to the *Barracuda*. Moments later he was on the bridge. "I have the CONN," he told the officer at the COMCOMP. Then he switched on the MC. "Deck detail stand by to retrieve all lines."

"Standing by, Skipper," the chief signaled.

Borodine said something over the *Sea Dragon*'s MC and the lines holding the two ships together were slipped from the cleats.

"Take in all lines," Boxer said.

"Aye, aye, Skipper," the chief answered.

Almost immediately the two ships drifted apart.

Still on the open MC, Borodine gave two swift orders that brought most of the *Sea Dragon*'s crew on deck. Switching to English, Borodine said, "Comrade Admiral Boxer and the crew of the *Barracuda*, we wish to salute you."

"We will take your salute as soon as my men are assembled," Boxer answered; then switching the operation of the *Barracuda*, he ordered the crew to assemble on the forward deck.

Dawson keyed him. "With your permission, Admiral, I would prefer not to take part —"

"On deck Colonel," Boxer growled. "Now!"

"Yes, sir," Dawson responded.

Boxer switched on the MC. "Comrade Admiral Borodine, my men are ready," he said.

Borodine barked out an order.

The men on the deck of the *Sea Dragon* came to attention.

Boxer called his crew to attention.

Borodine ordered his men to salute.

The crew of the *Barracuda* returned the courtesy.

Borodine told his men to stand at ease.

"At ease," Boxer said over the MC.

Then Borodine said, again speaking in English, "Many times we have been the hunter and the hunted. That is what our governments expect us to do. But there were times when something more than our mission took control of what we did. That something brought you to the *Sea Dragon* at a time when, if you had not come, neither I or any of my crew would be alive. It is fitting therefore for all of us aboard the *Sea Dragon* to salute you as comrades."

"All of us aboard the *Barracuda*," Boxer said, speaking over the MC, "know that if the situation had been the reverse, you and your men would have come to our aid. That 'something' you spoke about has as one of its parts a mutual respect."

Borodine called his men to attention; then dismissed them.

"Atten-hut," Boxer said and a moment later, he added, "Dismissed."

Borodine and Viktor waved.

"All hands now hear this," Boxer said, "all hands stand by to get underway… Switching from AUTOCONTROL to MANUAL.… Stand by."

"All systems green," Cowly reported.

"Roger that," Boxer answered; then keying the EO, he said, "Give me two-zero knots."

"Going to two-zero knots," the EO responded.

Boxer looked at Cowly. "Twelve days should see us home," he said, "and that's with a few deep dive tests along the way."

Cowly grinned. "That sounds good to me, Skipper."


"The son-of-a-bitch has done it," Mason roared, pacing the length of his office. "He's given the Russians back." Mason's naturally red face turned shades darker. He paused at his desk to pick up an already lit cigar from the ashtray and began puffing on it. He was a heavy set man with small brown eyes and a bald head. "By Christ, I'll have him up on charges!"

Tysin shook his long head. "No, you won't."

Mason stopped and took the cigar out of his mouth. "Why the hell not? He disobeyed my orders. He disobeyed your orders."

"The President won't let you court-martial a man to whom he recently gave a Congressional Medal of Honor."

"What the fuck does that have to do with it?"

"His image would be damaged," Tysin answered.

Mason began to pace again. "I'll talk to him."

"I already have," Tysin said. "He won't budge on this one and you know that once he digs his heels in on an issue he's worse than a goddamn mule."

Mason stopped. "Then you tell me what we're going to do with a man who's not a team player."

"Get him off the team," Tysin said, launching himself out of the chair. "I won't put up with a maverick the way Kinkade did. I don't have a granddaughter whom I have to protect."

"Is it true she had the Russian —"

Tysin cut him short. "Boxer is out," he said.

"It's one thing to say it; it's another thing to do it. Tell me how you're going to get him out?"

"First," Tysin said, "I just don't mean out of the Company. I mean completely out."

Stopping, Mason asked, "Dead?"

Tysin nodded. "Yes, if it comes to that."

Mason puffed hard on the cigar. The pale, gaunt-looking man standing in front of him was a lot more dangerous than he would have thought. "How?" he asked.

"I know people who have scores to settle with him. Morell for one, and Sanchez for another."

"Sanchez? I thought he and Boxer were tight?"

"The operative word is 'were' and that connotes the past. I know for a fact that when Boxer was in Italy he screwed up a deal for Sanchez which, by the way, was part of an ongoing joint business venture between the Company and Sanchez. So we lost out and so did Sanchez and that's something that greatly displeases him."

"Enough to kill him?"

"Yes, I would think so," Tysin answered.

For several moments, neither of them spoke; then Mason said, "The *Barracuda* returns in ten days, twelve at the very most."

"Chi-Chi," he cautioned, "this is one operation we can't afford to rush. We'll let it simmer awhile. If it fails and our names become linked with it, we're finished. Not even the President will be able to protect us."

"Not even if it was done to protect our national security?"

Tysin shook his head. "Not even then," he answered slowly. "On this one we'll be out on a limb together and if someone should saw off the limb — well, we'll probably get twenty-five years."

Mason went back to the desk and put the cigar back in the ashtray. "I need a drink," he said. "What about you?"

"I wouldn't mind a scotch on the rocks," Tysin answered. "But not here."

Mason looked at his watch. "It's almost midnight."

"On second thought," Tysin said, "I'll take a rain check on that drink. Tomorrow is Saturday and I have to be up early for a Little League game."

"The pleasures of fatherhood," Mason commented. "I'm glad I never experienced it with any of my three ex-wives."

Tysin walked to the door, stopped before he reached it and looking back at Mason, he said, "I'll start the ball rolling. I don't want this to get away from us."

This was the second time in five days that Borodine and Polyakov were meeting face to face. They met for the first time aboard the carrier *Minsk* before the landing. Now they were aboard the cruiser *Moskva*, where Polyakov occupied the captain's quarters.

Borodine was very tired. He sat on a simple, straight back, wooden chair in front of Polyakov's desk.

For several moments, Polyakov remained silent. He was a big, blond-headed man, with a clean shaven chin, blue eyes, and a sensuous mouth. He took time to snip off one end of a cigar and light the other; then he said, "The *Sea Dragon* will accompany the cruisers *Moskva* and *Leningrad* to Kronstadt."

Borodine had no objection. He nodded.

"At no time during the voyage home will you be more than a thousand yards from each cruiser… You keep a position between them."

Borodine's eyebrows went up; his stomach tightened. But he remained silent.

"At no time during the voyage home will you order a dive," Polyakov said.

Borodine leaped to his feet. "I must test dive —"

"Sit down!" Polyakov snapped.

Borodine glared at him. "May I remind you, Comrade Admiral, that we hold the same rank and that the operation is over."

"You and your entire crew are under arrest," Polyakov said. "I have ordered the captains of the *Moskva* and *Leningrad* to destroy the *Sea Dragon* should you disobey my orders."

Borodine sucked in his breath and slowly exhaled. In extreme situations the naval regulations permit the arrest of one officer by another.

"I have drawn up a document of charges against you and your crew, which include crimes against the state."

"You must be crazy!" burst out of Borodine.

Suddenly Polyakov pointed his finger at Borodine and began shouting, "I hold you and your crew responsible for the operation's failure. Everything was planned to perfection.

Whatever went wrong, went wrong because you and your crew failed to carry out your orders."

"Polyakov," Borodine said stiffly, "this matter will be settled in Moscow. But I will tell you this: unless the orders come from Moscow to the contrary, I will command the *Sea Dragon*. Do not make the mistake of exceeding your authority."

Polyakov's face turned pale. His lower lip trembled.

"I warned you not to underestimate Boxer," Borodine said. "The failure for the operation rests squarely on your shoulders."

"Not so," Polyakov roared. "The plan was flawless."

"A plan is only a plan."

Polyakov started to stand; then changing his mind, he sat down again. "You should have destroyed the *Barracuda*."

"I came close to doing it; then the fire broke out."

For several moments neither of them spoke; then Borodine said, "The *Sea Dragon* will proceed alone to its home port."

"I will bring charges against you," Polyakov told him.

Borodine nodded. "To protect yourself, you must."

"I won't respond to that. But you must realize that even if you are not found guilty, there will always be the suspicion in some circles that you might have been."

"That's assuming I go to trial."

"Even if you don't, your career will be finished."

Borodine shrugged. "That's a chance I'll have to take, isn't it?"

Polyakov didn't answer. He looked down at the papers on the desk.

"Before I leave," Borodine said, "I want to give you something to think about, Comrade Admiral."

Polyakov raised his eyes.

"Two things," Borodine said. "The first is that by destroying me, you might very well destroy yourself. Remember, you were willing to abandon the assault force on the beach and it was you who decided that the *Tsindelis* should be used as bait."

"The plan —"

"Hear me out, Comrade Admiral," Borodine snapped. "The second has to do with the fact that you have a close personal relationship with the Premier's daughter, and therefore, a much closer relationship to people who are in a position to help your career. Even the way you came by this command might come into question. Certainly, you were not qualified or sufficiently experienced to lead this kind of operation."

Polyakov's face reddened. "My personal life has no connection with my professional —"

"Comrade Admiral," Borodine said, "in our society such connections will have enormous impact on the outcome of any trial; mine or yours."

"My trial?" Polyakov shouted, leaping to his feet. "What do you mean by 'my trial'?"

"I will answer your charges against me with charges against you," Borodine replied calmly. "Did you think that I wouldn't?"

Polyakov gripped the edge of the desk so tightly his knuckles turned white. "But that could force the Premier to resign," he said in a hoarse whisper.

"That's one of the risks you'll have to take, isn't it?"

Polyakov didn't answer.

"Comrade Admiral," Borodine said, "the real difference between us is that you're used to fighting for position and power, while I'm used to fighting for my life and the lives of my crew."

The two men stared at each other; then Polyakov picked up the document of charges and holding it out in front of him, he slowly began to tear it apart.

Borodine nodded. "A wise choice, Comrade Admiral. It will save the two of us a lot of trouble."

"Make no mistake," Polyakov told him, "I will make your destruction a personal project. I will —"

"Yes, I know you will try," Borodine said. "But believe me, I will not lose any sleep over it, especially since I have had first-hand experience with the results of your plans."

Polyakov turned pale again.

"An interesting meeting, Comrade Admiral," Borodine said and snapping a salute, he turned and walked as nonchalantly as he could to the door.

# CHAPTER 4

Boxer switched on the MC. "All hands now hear this... Now hear this... Stand by to surface... Stand by to surface! All systems on AUTOCONTROL... Helmsman, stand by."

"Helmsman standing by," Mahony answered.

"Switching to night lighting," Boxer said and an instant later the normal lighting diminished and an eerie red glow took its place.

Boxer checked the DDRO. The ship was down two hundred feet. His eyes moved to the AUTONAV and saw his position in terms of latitude and longitude. "Zero-five miles off the Chesapeake," he called out to Cowly.

"On chart," Cowly answered.

"Roger that," Boxer said and changed the position AUTODIV switch to AUTOSURFACE, NORM. Instantly, a battery of amber indication lights came on and one by one turned to green as each phase of the surfacing operation was initiated and successfully completed.

The SO keyed Boxer. "Scope clear of targets, Skipper."

"Roger that," Boxer responded. He checked the DDRO. The *Barracuda* was up fifty feet. He keyed the COMMO. "Inform base that we'll be dockside in two hours."

"Aye, aye, Skipper," the COMMO responded; then he added, "Message coming through for you."

"Read it."

"Base wants to know if we need a tug?"

"Negative," Boxer answered.

"There's more, Skipper. Admiral Stark will meet you at dockside."

"Roger that," Boxer responded happily and then to Cowly, he said, "Stark will be at dockside."

"That's great!" Cowly exclaimed.

"From the last report I received," Boxer said, "I didn't think the man had a snowball's chance in hell. It'll be good to see him."

"All systems green," Cowly reported.

"Roger that," Boxer said and over the MC, he announced, "Passing through seven-five feet." Then he reached over to speed control and decreased the number of knots the boat was making from twenty to ten. Then he checked the COMCOMP's sonar display. It was still clear. He keyed the METO. "What do we have topside?" he asked.

"Heavy fog... Wind less than zero-two miles per... Current at four miles per... Water temp five-eight degrees... Air temp four-four degrees... Rain within the next hour, according to base METO. But I'll have a better fix on that as soon as our radar is operating."

"Roger that," Boxer answered.

Suddenly a bell began to ring and the red three-minute TIME TO SURFACE INDICATOR began to flash.

"Two-five feet," Boxer said over the MC. "Stand by to raise sail."

"Standing by to raise sail," Cowly answered.

"Bridge detail, stand by," Boxer ordered.

"Bridge detail standing by," the duty officer reported.

The TTSI turned green and the klaxon sounded.

"Raise sail," Boxer ordered.

"Raising sail," Cowly answered.

"Bridge detail, topside," Boxer said.

A half dozen men ran to the bridge hatchway, opened it and disappeared.

"Mahony to the bridge," Boxer ordered.

"Aye, aye, Skipper," Mahony answered.

Boxer ran a SYSCHEK. All systems were green. "Cowly, let's go topside," he said.

Despite the heavy fog, Boxer was glad to be out of the *Barracuda*. Though he managed to control his claustrophobia, he was never unaware of its presence.

The RO keyed him. "Skipper, I have eight targets in radius of twenty-five thousand yards. They're flying the lazy eight of a holding pattern. Do you want them tracked?"

"Negative, unless you want to give some of your men practice," Boxer answered. "Limit your reports to targets within a radius of five thousand yards."

"Aye, aye, Skipper," the RO answered.

"We should be seeing the lights of the bridge soon," Cowly commented.

"Mahony," Boxer called, "set the EHC on fog display."

"Aye, aye, Skipper," Mahony responded.

The RO keyed Boxer again. "Target, bearing seven-three degrees... Range, twenty-four thousand yards... Course, two-eight-eight degrees... Speed one-one knots... no ID."

Boxer checked the COMCOMP's surface radar display. "Take a look and tell me what you think," he said to Cowly.

"Could be a local fishing trawler."

"Could be," Boxer agreed. "But my gut feeling tells me it's one of our Russian friends." He keyed the COMMO. "On an open frequency call base and report a possible bogie tracking us, moving on two-eight-eight degree heading."

"Aye, aye, Skipper," the COMMO answered.

"If it's one of ours and picked up our message, its skipper should be on the air in a matter of minutes," Boxer said. "And if it's one of theirs —"

The RO keyed Boxer. "Target changing course… Bearing, seven-four degrees… Course twenty-six degrees… Increased speed to two-one knots."

"Roger that," Boxer answered, grinning.

"Just a good guess," Cowly said.

"A gut feeling."

"Skipper, the bridge just came up on the EHC," Mahony said.

"Roger that," Boxer answered; then looking at the COMCOMP's clock, he said, "We should be at dockside by twenty-two hundred."

"Can't be soon enough for me," Cowly said. "I miss Cynthia more than I would have believed I could."

"I know what you mean," Boxer answered.

Lowering his voice, Cowly said, "She has given me a whole new life. I never knew anyone like her before."

Boxer nodded.

"Skipper," Cowly said, "for the first time in years I'm a happy man. I don't have that gray feeling inside of me. I —"

"Do you hear something?" Boxer asked suddenly. "Off the port side?"

"Nothing — no, there's something out there."

Boxer flicked a toggle. The beam from the portside high intensity searchlight leaped into the fog and was quickly diffused.

"Nothing on radar," Cowly said.

"That fucking noise is getting louder" Boxer said. "Helmsman, over to nine-zero degrees."

"Going to nine-zero degrees," Mahony answered.

Suddenly Cowly pointed into the fog. "Holy Christ, it's coming straight at us!"

Boxer managed to hit the COMCOMP's red crash button seconds before an explosion sent a rush of flames over the deck. The *Barracuda* rolled to the starboard. A second explosion blew out the forward part of the bridge and the fire dropped down into the sail's well. Within moments a third explosion tore through the topside bridge.

Boxer keyed the COMMO. "Get a May Day out. Say we're on fire and have many casualties!"

"Aye, aye, Skipper," the COMMO answered.

Boxer looked at the bridge detail. Two men badly torn up. A third dead and Cowly had been thrown to the deck. Only he and Mahony were still on their feet. Boxer keyed the MO. "Casualties on the bridge," he said.

"Skipper, we've casualties all over the boat," the MO said. "I don't have enough men to take care of them."

"Roger that," Boxer answered, vaguely aware of the throb of engines off the stern.

The DCO keyed Boxer. "We're taking water amidship on the port side, we have a fire in the mess area and one in the engine room. Shutting down all air blower systems."

"Roger that," Boxer answered.

"Skipper," Mahony said, "Mister Cowly isn't moving."

Boxer hunkered down and bent over Cowly.

He was bleeding profusely from the back of his head.

Boxer's throat tightened. He clenched his teeth. There was nothing he could do for him. He fought back his tears and stood up. "Is the EHC operating?" Boxer asked.

"Yes," Mahony answered.

"Bring her close in to the shore," Boxer said. "I'll beach her."

"Aye, aye, Skipper," Mahony answered.

The COMMO keyed Boxer. "Help is on the way."

"Roger that," Boxer answered. He reduced the *Barracuda*'s speed to five knots.

Suddenly an explosion buckled a section of the aft deck. Flames shot through the opening of twisted steel.

The DCO keyed Boxer. "Fire in the engine room and mess area out of control! We're at one-five degree list to the port side."

"Roger that," Boxer answered, hearing the sound of an approaching chopper. "Mahony, how close are we to the shore?"

"Five hundred yards."

"Roger that," Boxer answered automatically.

"That chopper should be able to see us by now," Mahony commented.

Boxer didn't answer. Suddenly the FAIL SAFE ALARM went off and at the same time a panel of red lights on the power control section of the COMCOMP began to flash. The control rods had automatically closed the reactor down and four huge wet cell batteries now provided power for the *Barracuda*.

The DCO keyed Boxer. "Reactor out on battery power."

"Roger that."

"At the present rate of consumption we have at the most two hours' worth."

"Let's hope we won't need it that long."

"Ten-four, Skipper."

The Coast Guard chopper came down off the port side and hovered a few feet off the water. The wind from its rotor blew over the bridge. "What's your situation?" A voice asked over a PA.

Boxer switched on the MC. "On fire… Listing to the port side… Many casualties."

"Has your reactor shut down?"

"Yes," Boxer answered.

"Can you beach?"

"Should be able to."

"Will you abandon ship?"

"Negative," Boxer answered firmly.

"Heave to," the voice from the chopper said. "Two cutters are coming toward you."

"Roger that," Boxer answered and he reduced the *Barracuda*'s power to zero. Then he said, "Radar is out… Fire out of control in the engine room and mess area… I have many dead and injured."

"Ten-four," the voice answered.

The COMMO keyed Boxer. "Admiral Mason and Mr. Tysin are on their way here. They're on the Navy tug *Bascomb*."

"Roger that," Boxer said.

Suddenly a head appeared over the bridge railing. It was one of the ship's corpsmen.

"It's the only way to get up here, Skipper," the man explained. "Everything inside the sail is twisted up."

"I have two dead and four badly hurt," he said. The corpsman saw Cowly, looked at Boxer and shook his head. "Sorry, Skipper, I know he was a good friend."

"The best," Boxer managed to say in a choked voice.

"I'll check the others out," the corpsman said.

Boxer nodded and turned away just as one of the cutters broke out of the fog.

Boxer and several volunteers, including Mahony, the COMMO and the DCO remained aboard the *Barracuda* until all the injured and dead were taken off, the fires out and the boat was safely secured to the tugs *Bascomb* and *Whitney*.

When Boxer and the men with him finally joined Mason and Tysin in the tug's mess area, it was two o'clock in the morning.

"I'll be with you in a few minutes," Boxer told Mason and Tysin. He went straight to the coffee urn. "You men help yourselves," he said. "I see there's sandwiches and doughnuts." He took a ham sandwich and biting into it, he walked to where Mason and Tysin were standing.

"We'll need preliminary statements," Tysin said.

Boxer looked back at his men. Their faces were smudged with grime and smelled of smoke. He knew that like himself, they were exhausted physically and mentally. His first impulse was to say, *no*. But instead he said, "Don't make it a long session. The men are beat."

"We'll be as brief as we can," Tysin answered. "I have men coming out with tape recorders."

Boxer nodded and dropped down on one of the benches.

"What the hell happened out here?" Mason asked.

Boxer screwed his eyes up. "My best guess is that a high-speed motorboat collided with the *Barracuda*." He lowered his eyes and said, "My best guess is that it was no accident."

"Are you suggesting that the Russians —" Tysin began.

"I am not suggesting the Russians," Boxer answered.

"But you said —"

"I know fucking well what I said and I didn't say anything about the Russians."

The MO approached Boxer. "Skipper, I request permission to return to the base hospital with our injured. They'll feel better if they see me around."

"Your wife and kids will be waiting for you," Boxer said. He knew the MO was married and had three children.

The MO nodded. "The men need me more than my wife and kids do," he said. "As long as I can call them and they know I'm safe, they'll be able to wait a little longer to see me."

Boxer nodded. "Go up to the wheelhouse and tell the captain that you have my permission to use the radio phone."

"Thanks, Skipper," the MO said.

Boxer nodded and picking up the coffee mug, took several sips.

"Admiral Stark and Ms. Wheeler are waiting for you at the base," Mason told him.

"Cowly, my EXO, is dead," Boxer said. "I'll appoint an acting EXO. He'll be the same man I want to take Cowly's place."

"That can wait," Tysin said.

Boxer looked up at Mason. "Does Mister Tysin command the fucking ship or do I?"

"Make your appointment," Mason responded.

Tysin's face remained expressionless. "You made your point, now I'll make mine. The press was informed about the accident and they will be waiting on the dock. Neither you or your men are to make any statement to them beyond the requisite, 'No comment.' Is that understood?"

Boxer wearily pulled himself to his feet. "I want another cup of coffee and I want to speak to my men."

"Do you understand what I just said?" Tysin asked.

"Neither I nor my men will say any more to the press than is necessary," Boxer answered.

"I don't want you to say anything."

"That's going to be a problem," Boxer answered.

"This is a matter of national security."

Boxer shook his head and he went to the coffee urn, filled his mug; then facing the men in the crowded mess area, he said in a loud voice, "Listen up, men."

The galley was immediately silent.

"There's no need for me to tell you how I feel about you. But in case you'd like to hear it: you're the best damn crew a skipper could have. The best!

"Admiral Mason and Mister Tysin must have preliminary statements from all of you about the accident. These statements will be taped and you will not be kept longer than is absolutely necessary. When we reach dockside, I will have special phone lines set up for you.

"Any questions?"

"Skipper," one of the men said, "if the hospital needs blood for our guys, all of us are ready to give."

"Thanks," Boxer said. "I'll let you know when we're dockside."

"Skipper," Mahony called out, "we want Admiral Mason and Mister Tysin to know that you're the best skipper in the whole damn Navy. Isn't that right guys?"

"Sure as hell is," several of the men called.

"Fuckin' all right," another group sang out.

"He's number one!" a third group said.

Boxer flushed. "Okay guys," he told them, "you know that's not scoring any brownie points with me."

The men laughed and one of them answered, "Skipper, there's not a man here who doesn't owe you his life. There's not a man here —"

Boxer held up his free hand and looking at Mason and Tysin, he said, "I think they've gotten the idea." Then he nodded to his crew, left the urn and returned to the table where he had been sitting.

"I'm still not sure I understand what you meant when you said that the crash was deliberate," Tysin said.

"I didn't use the word deliberate. I said it wasn't an accident."

"Listen Boxer," Tysin said, "I do not like your attitude or your tone."

Boxer stood up. "And I certainly don't like yours," he said and started to walk away.

Mason called him back. "I'll assume you're overwrought," he said, "and that ordinarily you would not behave in a manner unbecoming of an officer and a gentleman."

"Don't assume anything, Admiral," Boxer said. "I am indeed overwrought, but not to the degree that I don't know what I'm doing. Now, if you'll excuse me, I have to go to the head." And turning around, he walked quickly away.

Tysin and Mason moved outside of the mess area and were standing on the stern. Both men had their hands dug deep into their coat pockets and Tysin walked in a tight circle before he said, "The man is insufferable. But this will be the beginning of his end."

"I don't understand," Mason said.

"A Court of Inquiry is usually convened to investigate the accident."

"That's right."

"This one will recommend that Admiral Boxer, captain of the *Barracuda* at the time of the accident, was guilty of gross negligence and should be tried by a court-martial."

"You can't be sure —"

"You can appoint officers to the board who are hungry for advancement. You can hint that you're looking for very specific recommendations. I'm sure there are many officers in the Navy who are more than a little jealous of Boxer and would like to see him cut down."

"Are you telling me —"

"Mason, that man is as much a thorn in your side as he is in mine. You want to get rid of him and so do I. This collision has given us the perfect chance. We won't have another one like it."

"Then Boxer was right; it wasn't an accident?"

Tysin didn't answer.

"I thought you'd do it another way," Mason said.

"I don't know what you're talking about," Tysin said. "But now we have the opportunity to accomplish what both of us want."

Mason pulled out a cigar case from his breast pocket and removed a cigar. After it was cut and lit, he said, "It could be done, with the board, I mean."

"I was sure it could. And with the court-martial too."

Mason puffed on the cigar. "Yes, with the court-martial, too."

Suddenly the captain of the tug came on the PA. "We're approaching dockside. Stand by. Deck detail at your places."

Boxer stood up and walked out on deck. The brightly illuminated pier lay about thirty yards off the bow. There were a half-dozen black limos visible and three TV networks had their white trucks there.

The skipper of the tug cut the two huge diesel engines and let the forward thrust take the ship closer to the dock. Then he turned the right propeller over a few dozen revolutions and that brought the tug parallel to the concrete pier.

"Bow and stern lies out," the captain ordered over the PA.

The thin lines were tossed to receivers on the pier and one inch hawsers were pulled onto the dock and quickly double-eighted around the cleats.

"Gangway out," the captain said.

The tug's searchlights suddenly went out and a swarm of TV people rushed toward the ship.

The high intensity lights were in his eyes, blinding him as the microphones were thrust close to his face.

One reporter said, "Admiral, is there anything you want to say about the disaster?"

"Only that my heartfelt sympathy goes out to the relatives and sweethearts of the men who were killed," Boxer said.

"Can you give us any details about the accident?" another reporter asked.

"All the information you want will be released in an official statement from the Navy," Boxer answered.

Suddenly Boxer found himself looking at Ms. Johnson. Before he became serious with Francine, he almost had an affair with her. His first claustrophobic attack had come in her apartment.

"Are you sure, Admiral, you were in control of the situation at the time of the attack?" she asked.

"I'm not sure I understand the question," Boxer said.

"That at the time of the accident, or immediately prior to it, you were in complete possession of your faculties."

Boxer's heart skipped a beat and began to race. "If you're asking whether or not I was in command of the *Barracuda*, I had the CONN."

She smiled sweetly at him and said, "Admiral, you know that was not exactly what I was referring to."

Another reporter came to his rescue by asking, "Could you tell us how many casualties there were?"

"I'm sorry, I can't. There will be an official statement after the next of kin have been notified," Boxer said; then he added, "Now if you will excuse me, I am very tired."

A group of Marine MPs cleared a path for Boxer to the limo, where Stark and Francine were waiting. He slid down beside Francine, took her in his arms and kissed her on her lips; then he let go of her and shaking Stark's hand, he said, "Hello, Admiral. Thanks for coming to meet me." Even by the dim light of the limo, he could see how frail Stark had become.

"Nothing," Stark said. "Wouldn't have missed it." His voice was still gravelly. But now it also had a slight slur.

"Are you all right?" Francine asked, holding tightly to his arm. Before he could answer, she said, "I was so worried. We weren't told anything. We were just told that there had been an accident and that there had been casualties."

"Cowly is dead," Boxer said softly.

"On no!" Francine cried.

Stark couldn't find his voice and when he did, he said, "We'd better stop at the house and tell Cynthia, if she doesn't already know."

Boxer picked up the intra-phone and gave the driver the Cowly's address.

"Why don't you have a drink, Jack?" Stark suggested. "You look as if you could use one."

"I'll fix it for you," Francine said and releasing Boxer's arm, she leaned forward and opened the small bar that was fitted into the rear of the front seat.

"Make it a double," Boxer told her; then he leaned back and closed his eyes. "I think I could sleep for a year," he commented.

Francine placed the drink in his hand.

"I almost lost the *Barracuda* in a tsunami off the coast of the People's Republic of Yemen," he said. "I tried to run under it and wound up being almost smashed to pieces by boulders moving at hundreds of miles an hour." He opened his eyes and took several swallows of the vodka. "That tastes good," he commented. Then he said, "Borodine sends his best to you, Admiral."

Stark smiled.

"He had a fire aboard his ship that almost killed him and everyone else," Boxer said.

"You'll talk about it another time," Stark told him. "Now you had better save whatever energy you have left for your meeting with Cynthia."

"That sure as hell isn't going to be easy," Boxer said and finishing the vodka, he handed the glass to Francine. "Will you fix me another, please?" Then he said, "I never did ask how either of you are."

"I'm fine," Francis said, handing the glass back to him. "This time it's not a double."

Boxer nodded. "Admiral, what about you?"

"Better than I thought I'd be a few weeks back," Stark said. "I'm not fit for sea duty, or for that matter any kind of duty. But I somehow managed to pull myself around."

"Pull yourself around," Francine chided. "Jack, he won't stay put. I mean, he insists on going shopping. He even runs the vacuum around."

"Sounds as if the two of you are the odd couple," Boxer said.

"We are. She's worse than a mother hen," Stark complained. "But now that you're here —"

"Wait a minute," Boxer exclaimed. "I'm confused!"

"It's very simple," Francine said, "I wasn't about to let Admiral Grouch live alone and kill himself; so in a moment of insanity, I convinced him to live with me."

"Admiral Grouch?" Boxer questioned; then with a nod, he said, "I like it. It somehow fits." And giving Francine's knee a squeeze, he added, "Thanks for taking care of him."

"I assure you," Stark told him, "that I took care of her as much as she took care of me. That woman would never stop working if it wasn't for me. I had to take her by the hand and drag her away from the desk."

Boxer finished his second drink, before he said, "And thank you, Admiral, for taking care of her. I'd squeeze your knee too, but —"

The intra-phone rang and Boxer answered it.

"Admiral, we'll be at the house in a few minutes," the driver said.

Boxer thanked him and told Francine and Stark, who said, "Even if she hasn't yet received official notification, she might know. She has a great many contacts in the department."

"We'll soon find out," Boxer responded.

And as they turned onto the street where the Cowlys' house was located, none of them spoke until Francine said, "There are lights on downstairs and a couple of cars parked in the driveway."

They pulled up in front of the house and stopped.

The driver got out and opened the door on the side where Boxer was sitting.

"I'd better do this alone," Boxer said.

"Are you sure?" Francine asked.

Boxer took hold of her hand. "A few years back," he said, "Cynthia and I were lovers."

"I didn't know," Francine responded in a whisper.

Boxer leaned over and kissed her forehead. "If I need either of you, I'll come and get you," he said, as he left the car. He walked up to the door and twice in rapid succession he stabbed the bell button with his forefinger.

Inside the house chimes sounded.

A few moments passed and he was about to push his finger against the bell button again, when the door opened and he found himself looking at a petite woman, wearing a lounging robe and a nightgown under it.

"I'm Anna Cross. I live in the house next door," she explained, stepping back.

Boxer nodded and gave her his name.

Anna nodded. "Cynthia told me all about you. She was sure you'd come tonight."

"Where is she?"

"In the living room," Anna said, closing the door.

Boxer pursed his lips. "How is she?"

Anna shrugged. "Holding everything in," she said.

Boxer took a deep breath and as he slowly exhaled, he started to walk toward the living room.

"I think she was waiting for you," Anna said.

Boxer didn't respond. He stopped in the doorway of the living room.

Cynthia was seated on the couch between two women. Another woman occupied a blue club chair opposite the couch. A man was pouring a drink at the wagon bar and two others were standing and talking near the doorway that led to the dining room. This was the second time that Boxer had been at the house. The first time was for the housewarming a few days before the *Barracuda* sailed for its sea trials. Now there was more of a feeling of a home to it than there had been then. Cowly would have enjoyed coming back to it.

"Jack!" Cynthia suddenly exclaimed and started out of the chair.

Boxer immediately went to her.

She flung her arms around his neck and embraced him fiercely.

He kissed her.

She stepped away from him and speaking to everyone in the room, "People, this is Admiral Boxer, Bob's skipper."

Boxer nodded.

Cynthia took hold of his hand. "Drink?" she asked.

"No, thank you," he said. "I already had two in the limo coming here. Stark and Francine send their condolences."

"Are they waiting for you?"

Boxer nodded. "They came down to the dock."

"Before Bob left he told me not to meet him. He wanted to come home to this house. He loved —" Her voice faltered, but she quickly found it again and said, "He loved this place." She looked away.

"It's all right to cry," Boxer told her.

"I loved him," she said. "I really loved him."

Boxer remembered the times they had spent together. She was a beautiful woman, with long hair the color of wheat and sky blue eyes. "And he loved you," Boxer responded.

"He told you that?"

"Yes, just before he was killed."

"You were with him?"

"Both of us were on the sail's bridge when it happened," Boxer said and suddenly he was back on the bridge. The RO had just finished reporting the position of the target and several moments later the first explosion occurred. The target couldn't have covered the remaining distance between it and the *Barracuda* in that short time span. That means that no collision took place, but something struck the *Barracuda*. Something — It had to be a missile, a low flying missile!

"Jack are you all right?" Cynthia asked.

"Yes… Yes… I'm sorry," he said, looking at her. "I just remembered something that happened."

With her hand, she touched the side of his face. "The next few weeks aren't going to be easy for you."

"You know the drill. There must be a Board of Inquiry and it will make its recommendations."

"Jack, I know you can't tell me what happened and if I knew, it wouldn't mean anything to me. But I would feel better, if I knew —"

"He didn't suffer, if that's what you want to know."

"Thank you. I won't ask for details," she said softly.

He put his arm around her waist. "Thank you. I don't think I could give them. Bob was a very good friend. No, I'll say he was my best friend."

"You know you were his?"

"Yes," Boxer said.

"He never asked about us," she said. "He never asked about the other men in my life. The first time we made love he said to me, 'I love you, that's all that matters.' And that's all that did matter to him and to me."

"You gave him a great deal of happiness," Boxer said.

"He gave me the same," she answered.

"I'll be going now," Boxer said. "But I'll be back and if you need anything, I'm not more than a phone call away and if you need legal help, speak to Francine."

She wrapped her arm around his. "I'll walk you to the door."

"No need to," Boxer told her. "But if I were you, I'd get some sleep. The next few days are going to be tough ones."

She disengaged her arm from his. "Jack, what am I going to do without him?" she asked in choked voice. "I know I didn't really spend much time with him, but he gave me everything I ever wanted."

"Survive," Boxer said with a sigh. "Survive."

"Hold me."

He hugged her tightly.

"Now go to Francine," Cynthia said, "before I become weepy."

Boxer kissed her on her lips and walked quickly to the door. Moments later, he settled down in the rear seat of the limo next to Francine again and leaning his head back, he closed his eyes.

"Difficult?" she asked in a whisper.

"Difficult," he breathed.

"Let's go home," Francine said.

"I'm still waiting for Cowly's death to impact on me," Boxer said. "I'm still expecting to see him and hear his voice."

Stark and Francine remained silent and after a few moments, Boxer said, "Something is wrong. Admiral, the entire sequence of events came back to me while I was speaking to Cynthia."

"You're not making much sense," Stark told him.

Boxer opened his eyes and lifting his head, he looked at Stark. "The *Barracuda* wasn't involved in a collision."

"But that's what we were told."

"And that's what I believed until a few minutes ago."

"Then what did happen?" Francine asked.

"We were struck by a low flying missile," Boxer answered.

"Christ, are you sure?" Stark asked.

"Yes, very sure," Boxer said.

"Then it could have been the Russians after all."

"Could have been," Boxer admitted.

"They could have used a light plane —"

"There was nothing in the air. The air search radar screen was empty and so was the surface screen until we were practically on top of the target. It wasn't there and then it was coming at us. I took evasive action. But it kept coming; then came the first explosion and within seconds there was a second explosion. Cowly was killed by the second explosion. It threw him to the deck. The back of his head was split open."

Francine uttered a wordless cry.

"We'll talk more about this after you've had some sleep," Stark said. "You have to be very careful about what you say. If it turns out to be the Russians, the President might be pressured into asking Congress for a declaration of war, or worse, he might be pressured by various people to make a pre-emptive strike."

"I want to go down to the shore house," Boxer said. "I won't be able to relax here in Washington. I've got to try to figure out what kind of vessel was used to launch the missile."

"Are you sure it was a missile?" Stark asked.

"Absolutely sure," Boxer answered, sitting up and looking at Stark. "There's no doubt in my mind that it was a fucking missile!"

Stark nodded. "I believe you," he said.

Boxer uttered a weary sigh and relaxed against the back of the seat again.

A floor lamp in the corner of the bedroom cast a soft white glow on the ceiling; and in the space around it there was a circle of light whose intensity greatly diminished at its circumference that reached almost to the door and extended out over the bed where Boxer lay waiting for Francine to join him.

The room was familiar to him, but he was aware that there were several new things in it. The floor lamp in the corner was one, a home entertainment center was another and the third was Rugger's nude painting of Francine, which was now enhanced by a simple walnut frame and hung on the wall to the right of the bed.

Wearing nothing more than a white diaphanous negligee, Francine entered the bedroom.

"Stop!" Boxer exclaimed.

She halted and asked, "What's this all about?"

"You're just beautiful," he said. "The light goes through your gown and makes your body glow."

"That's why I had to stop?"

"Yes," Boxer said, coming to a sitting position.

"Now, may I please continue?" she asked.

Boxer nodded. He enjoyed looking at her. She had high cheekbones, sensuous lips, very green eyes and long red hair, which she let loose around her shoulders. Her breasts were melon shaped and each nipple was light pink. She had a small, beautifully shaped ass, a narrow waist, good hips and graceful legs.

When she reached the side of the bed, she said, "You have a wolfish look."

"I was afraid it would show," he answered opening the negligee.

Francine slipped the garment off.

Boxer threw back the covers and made room for her. "You smell good," he said, as soon as she was settled next to him.

"I was so frightened you wouldn't come back," she whispered. "And when I was told about the accident, I was afraid that you had been killed. Oh Jack, I —"

He pressed his lips to hers.

"I love you," he said. "I missed you terribly."

Francine pressed herself tightly against him. "You warned me it would be difficult, but I had no idea of just how difficult it really was. I felt as if I had suddenly become half a person. Do you know what I mean?"

Boxer didn't try to answer. He caressed her hair. "Anything interesting happen while I was away?"

"I had Chuck fly down here one weekend and showed him the sights," she said.

"How did he react?"

"He enjoyed every minute of it," she said. "I have the necessary adoption papers drawn up. All you have to do is sign them and I'll submit them to the court."

"I'll go up and see him in a few days," Boxer said.

"I thought you wanted to go down to the shore?"

"I do. But I won't be able to go until after the Board of Inquiry is done and gives its recommendations."

Francine took hold of his hand and put it on one of her breasts. "I'll sleep better if you hold me."

He smiled. "Do we sleep with the light on?"

"There's an automatic switch," she said. "Reach up to the top of the headboard... Near the edge."

"Plastic?"

"Yes... Now press it... Voila, darkness!"

Boxer kissed her forehead.

"Is that all I get?" Francine asked.

"That's all I have the strength to give you now," Boxer said. "Besides, too much of a good thing is no good."

She giggled. "Whoever told you that lie?"

"A friend."

"He was no friend, if he told you that."

"Sure... Now go to sleep."

"Jack, I love you."

"And I love you," Boxer responded. "I love you very much."

She snuggled close to him. "Sleeping alone is the pits." She put her arm over his chest and the next moment she was asleep.

Boxer smiled, put his hands behind his head and stared at the ceiling. Tired as he was, he still wasn't able to sleep. He tried to remember everything that had happened immediately before the first explosion aboard the *Barracuda* and the more he thought about it, the more he seemed certain that there was a gap in his memory. Something didn't follow. He had heard the roar of a motor boat's engines become louder and louder; then when he saw it come out of the fog, he had increased speed and had ordered a full ninety-degree turn. The first explosion came moments later. Boxer pursed his lips. None of the salvage people mentioned anything about finding debris. There wouldn't be any, unless what was left of the boat sank after it struck the *Barracuda*. But if it was, as he thought, a missile that struck the boat, then there wouldn't be any debris.

Boxer's lids began to close and finally he slept, only to find himself on the *Barracuda*'s bridge again, hunkering down next to Cowly. This time when he saw what had happened to him, he wept.

"Jack, wake up," Francine called. "Jack, what's wrong?"

"Cowly," he sobbed, "Cowly is dead. My friend is dead…"

"Oh my darling," she exclaimed, taking him in her arms.

"He never had a chance," Boxer sobbed. "Never had a chance…"

# CHAPTER 5

Despite the fact that he had had only four hours of sleep, Tysin arrived at his office precisely at nine o'clock in the morning. He immediately switched on the intercom and said, "Ms. Collins, will you please come into my office."

"Yes, Mister Tysin," she answered.

Tysin nodded and switched off the intercom. Her voice was soft and had just a hint of a southern accent that made it pleasant to hear. Moments later, she entered the office. She was tall, svelte and had long black hair which reached her shoulders. Her eyes were black and by skillfully applying makeup, she enhanced them. She wore a blue, short skirt, stockings and a sheer white V-neck blouse through which Tysin could see her mini-white bra. According to her personnel record, her given name was Lori-Ann. She was twenty-six, a graduate of Boon College, having majored in political science. Her medical history indicated that she was healthy and the Company investigation of her indicated that, other than having two love affairs while she was at college, was presently involved with a young lawyer in the Justice Department.

Tysin gestured to the chair alongside the desk. "Please sit down," he said.

She sat down and crossed her legs. The hem of the blue skirt she wore went up, exposing a white thigh.

Tysin looked at her record. "You've been with us three months," he said.

"Yes."

"Your work is satisfactory. No, it's excellent, Ms. Collins."

"Thank you, Mister Tysin," she said.

"Have you ever thought of becoming one of us?" Tysin asked, fixing his pale blue eyes on her.

She raised her eyebrows.

"An agent," he said in a low, intense voice.

She uncrossed her legs, shifted her position and adjusted the hem of her skirt.

"I have to admit, I've thought about it," she said.

Tysin smiled and wagging his finger at her, he said, "I was almost sure you had, or I wouldn't have broached the subject to you."

She flushed, smiled and in a low voice, she asked, "I didn't think anyone noticed." She crossed her legs again.

"I noticed," he half lied. He had noticed her from the first day she had been assigned to him. She was young, beautiful and he was going on forty-five with a wife who was going through her menopausal changes. He couldn't help but notice her and fantasize what it would be like to make love to her.

She flushed again.

"If you agree, I will take care of the necessary paperwork," Tysin said. "Of course, you will have to go to school for several months before you are actually an agent."

"I understand that," she said.

"Then you do accept the offer, Ms. Collins?"

"Yes, I do."

"Excellent!" Tysin exclaimed.

"I really don't know how to thank you, Mister Tysin," she said.

He smiled. "May I call you Lori-Ann?" he asked.

"Lori would be fine," she answered.

"Lori… I like that name," Tysin said. "Lori, there is something you can do for me. It will give you some training before you actually start your formal course. But it must be kept strictly between us."

"It will... I swear it will."

Tysin nodded. "I believe you, Lori... I really do." He paused. "I want you to become friendly with Linda Johnson."

Lori looked blankly at him.

"Linda Johnson... Live At Five," Tysin said.

Lori smiled. "Now I know who you mean," she said.

"Good. Very good. I have arranged for you to lunch at the same restaurant where she lunches. I have also arranged for you to occupy an apartment on the same floor in the building where she lives."

"Must I actually stay there?" Lori asked.

"Absolutely," Tysin answered, knowing she was concerned about the reaction of her lover. "In fact you'll be giving a small party to which you will invite Ms. Johnson."

"What is the reason for all of this?" Lori asked.

"I want you to find out how well Ms. Johnson knows Admiral Boxer," Tysin said.

Lori uncrossed her legs again, but this time she didn't bother to adjust the hem of her skirt.

Tysin had difficulty keeping his eyes off her thighs and his thoughts away from what was tantalizingly close to being exposed.

"Why do all of this when you can just ask her?" Lori questioned.

Tysin put his palms against the edge of the desk. "This is a very sensitive situation," he said.

Lori shook her head. "That poor man," she said sympathetically. "I caught the news on TV this morning and saw pictures of him. He looked so sad, so very sad."

"The information that you will get is very important," Tysin told her. "It will help me protect Admiral Boxer."

"What makes you think that she has any information about the admiral?"

He smiled at her, reached out and put his hand on her stocking covered knee. "She does," he said.

Lori looked down at Tysin's hand but neither asked him to remove it, or made any move to do it herself.

"You will start your assignment today," Tysin said, taking a deep breath and slowly exhaling. "I want you to move into that apartment, or take sufficient clothes to give the impression that you're living there."

"What about furniture?"

"That will be taken care of this afternoon. Everything you need will be there."

"How long do I have?"

"As quickly as possible," Tysin said.

"Suppose she doesn't want to talk about Admiral Boxer?" Lori asked. She slowly uncrossed her legs and closed them. She still did nothing to remove his hand from her knee.

Tysin smiled. "You'll tell her that you and the admiral know each other, that for a short time you had an affair with him."

"With all due respect, Mister Tysin, she's not going to buy that," Lori said.

"Believe me, she will."

"Is there anything else?" Lori questioned, slightly parting her legs.

Tysin took another deep breath, exhaled and shaking his head, he moved his hand between her legs.

She looked at him but said nothing.

Tysin moved closer to her. His fingers caressed soft warm thigh. His throat and lips became dry.

"I'll lock the door," Lori said.

Tysin nodded and withdrew his hand from between her thighs. Half expecting her to bolt from the office, he watched her go to the door, lock it and start back across the room. He stood up and stepped away from behind the desk.

Lori came directly up to him. "Do you want me to undress?" she asked.

She was so close he felt the puffs of air when she spoke and the musky scent of her perfume completely surrounded him. He put his arms around her and drew him to her. Her body was soft and pliant. Her breasts pushed gently against his chest. He lowered his lips to hers and kissed her deeply.

She opened her mouth and played her fingers on the back of his neck.

His wife hadn't done either for years. Holding her young body so close to him filled him with pleasure.

"You didn't answer my question," Lori said. "Do you want me to undress?"

"Yes," he answered in a throaty whisper.

Lori smiled at him, eased herself out of his arms and took two steps back. "Would you like to do it?" she asked.

Tysin felt dizzy. Lori was wrapped in a haze. Before he could understand her question, he had to repeat it to himself. The mist in front of his eyes cleared and he said, "Very much."

"Let's move to the couch," Lori suggested.

Tysin nodded and followed her. He never had had sexual relations with a woman who had worked for him. The few times when he had become sexually involved, it always had happened away from the office and with a woman whom he'd never meet in his professional capacity. But the moment he had seen Lori, he had wanted her and this situation with Boxer had provided him with the perfect opportunity to seduce her.

Lori fluttered her eyelashes and teasingly said, "I hope you're not going to wear your jacket, Mister Tysin, while I'm in my birthday suit?"

Tysin smiled. "No. I assure you I won't." Then he said, "Calling me Mister Tysin is much too formal. When we're together like this," he told her, purposely choosing his words to gauge her reaction, "why don't you use my given name."

"Henry."

"I like the way you make it sound," he said, removing his jacket and putting it over a nearby chair.

"I like saying it," she responded. "It would be nice to say it again."

Tysin smiled. She had understood. He took her in his arms and kissed her passionately on the lips.

Tysin unbuttoned the front of her blouse and when it was completely open, he slipped the blouse off and undid her bra. Then he opened the button in the back of her skirt, pulled the zipper down and eased the skirt over her hips. It dropped to the floor.

Lori stepped out of its folds, picked it up and put it on the chair where Tysin had put her blouse and bra. "Why don't you start to undress," she said.

"Good idea," Tysin said with a laugh and he removed his tie and started to unbutton his shirt.

Lori took off her shoes and undid her stockings from the white garter belt she wore. "I'll leave my panties for you," she told him, taking off the garter belt.

Tysin nodded. He couldn't take his eyes off her. She was naked except for a pair of tight-fitting thin blue bikini briefs. Quickly, he stripped down to his shorts.

"You take mine off and I'll take yours off," Lori said, coming toward him.

Tysin pressed her against himself. He could feel her youth. It had a strength and vigor he had long forgotten existed. He closed his eyes and let himself be engulfed by the sensations that were flowing through his body.

Lori removed his shorts and he took her briefs off. Naked they embraced and moved to the couch. "It's a narrow place," Tysin said, suddenly realizing that it wasn't suited for the purpose.

"The floor?" Lori asked. "There's a lot of room there."

"I have no objections," Tysin said.

Tysin wasn't quite sure how it happened, but somehow he was on top of her. The sensation was so intensely exquisite, Tysin almost groaned. But instead he clenched his teeth and began to move.

Lori squirmed under him. "Yes… Yes… Ah, that's it… That's it." Her body tensed, arched and then shuddered.

Tysin eased himself up and looked at her. She was beautiful. Her breasts rose and fell with her deep breathing. Her eyes were closed and her head was to one side. He caressed her stomach; then becoming bolder, gently touched her breasts. She smiled. "I like that."

"And I like you," Tysin said, letting the words out before he could stop them.

She opened her eyes and looked at him. "You didn't have to say that. We're consenting adults."

"I wanted to say it," he told her, resting his hand on her right breast and squeezing it gently.

She put her hand over his. "Will you be able to visit me at the apartment?" she asked.

"Yes."

"Tonight?"

"No. I have another engagement. But tomorrow afternoon, around four."

Lori sat up, threw her arms around him and said, "I'm so happy it happened, Henry, between us… I'm so happy."

"So am I," Tysin answered, getting to his feet. "You can't imagine how much this means to me."

Lori offered him her hands and he pulled her up. She put her arms around him. "I think I can guess," she whispered.

"How?" he asked, pressing her naked body against his.

"By the way you looked at me every time you saw me."

"Was it that obvious?"

"To me it was," she said.

"Why?"

"Because I wondered about you too," she said.

"And now you know."

"I know that I want more of the same," Lori said.

Tysin kissed her hard on her lips. He knew he was a lucky man; he had found a woman to love before he was too old to make love. He caressed the back of her head. "Tomorrow afternoon at four."

"At four," Lori said, kissing him lightly on the forehead and freeing herself from his embrace. "Is it all right if I use your bathroom to freshen up?"

"Use anything you want," Tysin said.

She smiled at him, gathered her clothing together and disappeared into the bathroom, Tysin wanted to suggest they shower together. But decided he'd leave that for the following afternoon. There were so many, many things he wanted to do with her. Travel, go to the theater, walk hand in hand along a country road and make love. Make love…

The next morning Boxer was awakened by the smell of bacon and coffee. He put on a robe and hurried downstairs to the kitchen.

"Biscuits will be ready in a couple of minutes," Francine said without looking at him.

"Good. I didn't realize I was hungry," Boxer responded from the doorway.

"After the kind of work you did last night, I wouldn't doubt it," she said, turning the bacon.

"And what kind of work was that?" he asked, as he came up behind her. She was wearing a pair of blue jeans and an old flannel shirt. Her hair was swept up and set in a bun on the back of her head. He put his arms around her.

For several moments she leaned against him. "Work that needed doing," she said.

Boxer put his hands over her breasts and gently squeezed them. She wasn't wearing a bra.

"What are your plans for today?" she asked.

He let go of her. "I have to make a preliminary statement," he said, letting go of her and walking over to the table, where he sat down. A morning newspaper lay neatly folded next to the setting. He picked it up. Three-quarters of the front page was given over to the story of the accident. There was a picture of him and several of the crew. "Did you read the newspaper yet?" he asked.

"Yes. There isn't even a hint that you're at fault," she said, "if that's what you're worried about."

Boxer put the paper down. "Is the admiral awake?" he asked.

"Awake and gone for his morning constitutional," Francine answered. She looked at the clock on the opposite wall. "He should be back in fifteen or twenty minutes."

"Thanks for looking after him," Boxer said. "He's a very special man and very special to me."

"He said pretty much the same thing about you," Francine commented, opening the microwave oven, taking out a tray of biscuits and bringing it to the table.

Boxer sniffed. "You can't imagine how good that smells. Every bit of food aboard the *Barracuda* is dehydrated and when it is automatically prepared, it doesn't have any aroma. Everything is like that, except the cakes and pies the bakers prepare for us."

Francine returned to the stove. "Why are those any different?"

Boxer smiled. "Because the Navy said they would be freshly prepared. We don't have any cooks on board. Only two bakers and each of them has one assistant."

Francine removed the bacon from the frying pan and let it drain on a sheet of paper toweling. "Are you going to mention anything about the missile in your preliminary report?" she asked.

Boxer knew that she was looking at the question from a legal point of view. "I haven't decided," he answered.

"It might be wiser to wait until you're before the Board of Inquiry," Francine said, as she transferred the bacon from the toweling to a large plate. "How do you want your eggs?"

"Sunnyside up, flipped over and well done," Boxer said.

"Two?"

"Yes, please," he said; then he added, "I'm going to take a look around where the accident happened."

Francine turned around. "I don't understand."

"I'm going to dive and take a look at the bottom," he said, aware that the expression on her face had become taut. "I've got to know what's down there."

"Aren't the Navy divers going to do that?"

"Yes," Boxer said. "But I want to see things for myself."

"Are you going to mention that in your preliminary statement?"

Boxer shook his head. "It doesn't have any bearing on what happened out there. It's after the fact."

"What would happen if you didn't make mention of the missile today?" she asked.

"A preliminary statement is just that," Boxer answered. "It's to give the members of the Board of Inquiry a feel for what happened. The statements and the operational tapes will enable them to conduct their inquiry."

"What tapes?" Francine asked, approaching the table with a plate of bacon.

"Everything aboard is recorded. There are systems OP tapes and Command OP tapes."

She put the plate down and went back to the stove for the eggs. "I didn't know that," she said.

"It's in place to take care of a situation like this one," Boxer said, waiting until she sat down before he helped himself to a biscuit.

"Would the tapes have been able to record the sound of the missile?" she asked.

Boxer stopped buttering his biscuit and looked at her with new respect. By appearing to nonchalantly ask questions, she had made him reveal something very important.

She smiled at him. "If the missile's sound had been recorded, would you still have to dive?"

"If there's no debris down there and the tapes picked up the sound of the missile, then the board couldn't consider it an accident."

The front door opened and Stark entered the vestibule.

"Breakfast is on," Boxer called out.

"Good," Stark answered. "I worked up an appetite. It's getting chilly out there." He entered the kitchen and sat down.

"Francine suggested that the incoming missile might have been recorded on the OP tapes," Boxer said.

Stark helped himself to a biscuit.

"How do you want your eggs?" Francine asked, beginning to stand.

"Don't want any," Stark said in his gravelly voice. "A couple of biscuits, a couple of pieces of bacon and cup of coffee will do me fine." He looked at Boxer. "I made arrangements for you to dive late this afternoon. You have to get there before the Navy divers. They won't start until tomorrow morning. You've got to be sure there's nothing down there."

"That's what I told her," Boxer said, looking at Francine.

She pursed her lips. "It's just that I don't want you to do anything dangerous. I mean why put yourself in danger, when there's no need to?"

"There's every need," Stark said, "because he's already in more danger than you could imagine. Tysin and Mason will want his scalp, to say nothing about some of the congressmen and senators."

"But if it was an accident —"

"If it could be proved it was an accident," Stark said, "then it also might possibly be proved it was Jack's fault."

Francine didn't answer.

"We go out to the beach area by chopper," Stark said, neatly folding a strip of bacon on a half biscuit. "I've rented scuba gear from a place not far from here. You'll be diving about forty minutes before the tide goes out. That should give you enough time."

"There's about eighty feet of water there," Boxer said.

"Checked the charts," Stark responded. "Exactly eighty-two feet."

"You're not going alone, are you?" Francine asked. The rising pitch of her voice indicated her alarm.

Boxer nodded.

"If you thought about doing this, what makes you think that someone else is going to be doing the same thing?"

"She has a point," Stark said.

"Alone I'd have only me to worry about," Boxer said. "With someone else, I'd have —"

"The water down there is going to be murky as hell," Stark said. "Someone at fifty feet might not be a bad idea, if for no other reason than to keep the sharks away."

"Sharks!" Francine exclaimed.

"Always a possibility, at this time of year," Stark said.

"Any time of year," Boxer commented. "That bay is a big place and there's lot of food there for them."

"Then you certainly must go with someone," Francine said.

"It wouldn't be fair to call someone from the *Barracuda*," Boxer told them. "Those men have already been through enough."

"That young man, DB, would make the dive with you," Stark said.

Boxer nodded.

"Then call him, Jack," Francine said. "For my peace of mind, call him. Please." And reaching out, she capped his hand with hers.

"All right," Boxer answered. "I'll ask DB."

"Thanks," Francine whispered. "Thank you very much."

Tysin used a pay phone in the lobby of the Hilton. It took four rings before a man answered.

Without preliminaries the man said, "I was waiting for your call. I thought you'd call last night, or this morning."

"What the hell did you think you were doing?"

"The fucker has nine lives," the man said.

"You bungled the job," Tysin said.

"I told you I'd kill him and I will."

"You killed twenty-five men and injured a score more. That's what you did."

"I'll get him."

"Not yet," Tysin said. "It might look suspicious."

"When then?"

"When I tell you," Tysin answered. "Now we have to cover ourselves. A Navy diving team will be looking for wreckage tomorrow morning. I want them to find some."

"I'll get it done this afternoon," the man said.

"Here are the coordinates from the OP tapes," Tysin said and he gave the man the exact position of the *Barracuda* when the first explosion occurred. "It's accurate to the half-second," he told him.

"The wreckage will be scattered," the man said.

"How will you do it?"

"Blow up the motorboat," the man said.

"Make sure it's the one you used last night," Tysin said. "Boxer has to believe it was the motorboat he heard."

"It will be the same one," the man assured him.

"I'll be in touch," Tysin said.

The man didn't answer.

Tysin hung up, opened the telephone booth and for several moments stood there thinking about the situation he was orchestrating, but then his thoughts quickly switched to Lori and he was sorry he couldn't be with her that evening.

The *Sea Dragon* arrived in Kronstadt early on a cold, gray morning. By afternoon the entire crew boarded a plane and were flown to Moscow, where the first snow of the season had fallen the previous night and leaden skies and a biting north wind promised more within the next few hours.

Borodine was immediately ordered to report to Admiral Gorshkov, Admiral of the Fleet, at Naval Headquarters and the same order restricted the men to Moscow until further notice.

"Polyakov's doing," Viktor said, after Borodine had read the order to the men over the MC.

"A good guess," Borodine answered sourly. "More than half the crew live in places a thousand miles from here."

"Maybe it will only be for a couple of days," Viktor said.

"It shouldn't have been at all."

"I can't disagree with that," Viktor replied.

"I had better get going," Borodine said.

"Aren't you putting on your dress uniform?"

Borodine shook his head.

"At least take off the jumper," Victor said.

Borodine smiled. "I guess you're right. Those paper pushers at HQ would probably think I'm the janitor."

"Probably," Viktor agreed. "But if I were you, I wouldn't let my anger warp my judgment. The admiral just might be in a prickly mood and there might be someone with him."

Borodine frowned.

"You might as well dress as you should."

"I'd like to go bare-assed," Borodine said.

"You'd freeze your balls off before you ever got there," Viktor replied with a straight face.

The two men looked at one another; then exploded into laughter.

An hour later Borodine entered Gorshkov's office.

"Welcome home," Gorshkov said, rising from his chair and reaching across the desk to shake Borodine's hand. "Please sit down."

Borodine settled in the chair on the side of the desk.

"Cigar?" Gorshkov asked. He was a heavy set man with a ruddy complexion, a full head of gray hair and steel gray eyes.

"Yes, thank you," Borodine said.

Gorshkov opened the humidor on his desk and removed two cigars. "Have you changed from cigarettes to cigars?" he asked.

"No. I just happen to like your cigars."

Gorshkov did a double take, but he didn't speak again until after they were smoking. "Polyakov is here."

"Did he leave his ship?" Borodine asked, knowing that the *Sea Dragon* was four days ahead of the *Moskva* and the *Leningrad.*

"More than six days ago. He arranged to have both vessels make a courtesy call in Brest. From there he went to Paris and from Paris he flew home."

"It's marvelous how things can be arranged for you, if you are fucking the Premier's daughter," Borodine said, looking straight at his superior.

"He has demanded an official investigation of your conduct and the conduct of all the officers under your command," Gorshkov said.

Borodine blew a column of gray smoke toward the high ceiling. "The man is an idiot. Listen to the tapes and read my

117

report and you will come to the same conclusion, Comrade Admiral."

"He claims that you did not take any of the opportunities to destroy the *Barracuda* that presented themselves to you."

"What do you think, Comrade Admiral?" Borodine asked.

"It doesn't matter what I think," Gorshkov answered. "Polyakov will do everything in his power to break you and I can't do very much to stop him. I have power, as you well know I have. But his influence in political circles is probably as great as mine and at this moment there's a struggle going on in the Party."

Borodine pursed his lips. "Are you trying to tell me that I might be served up on a silver platter to prove something?"

Nodding, Gorshkov said, "Very possible."

"Then I and my officers are to be investigated?"

"There will be several hearings."

Borodine leaned forward. "Comrade Admiral, Comrade Admiral Polyakov was willing to abandon my men on the beach where they would have been killed if it were not for the fact that Comrade Boxer and I were able to work out an agreement."

"An agreement, I must remind you, that had neither my approval or his, and you were under his command."

Borodine moved back into the chair. He hadn't expected that kind of answer from Gorshkov. The Admiral of the Fleet had always supported him.

"Many people in and out of the service think that you should be taught a lesson," Gorshkov said, blowing smoke off to his right. "Many of the officers want other submarine captains to have the opportunity to command the *Sea Dragon*."

"I can understand the second part of what you just said," Borodine responded. "But as far as being taught a lesson —

118

well, Comrade Admiral, with all due respect to those who think that, I must say they have no idea what I and my men go through on any mission. I respectfully request that my officers and men be excused from —"

"They must appear at the hearings as ordered. What follows will depend on the recommendations that result from the hearings."

Borodine remained silent. He was sure that he no longer had the friendship or the backing of the man behind the desk.

"Comrade Admiral Boxer's ship was involved in an accident," Gorshkov said matter-of-factly.

Borodine started to stand; then immediately sat down again. "Where?" he asked in a low voice.

"At the entrance to the Chesapeake Bay. There were many casualties, but Comrade Admiral Boxer is alive. His EXO, who I think you also know, was killed."

"Cowly!" Borodine exclaimed. "Comrade Captain Cowly."

"Apparently the *Barracuda* was struck by a high-speed motorboat, the kind used by drug runners."

Borodine shook his head. "I must send a message of condolence to Comrade Admiral Boxer and the wife of Comrade Captain Cowly." He looked at Gorshkov and said, "If the situation was reversed, Comrade Admiral Boxer would do the same."

Gorshkov nodded, but he said nothing.

"Comrade Captain Cowly was recently married," Borodine commented. "I believe I met his wife before she became his wife."

"The hearings will commence in a few days," Gorshkov said. "You will be notified when and where to appear."

"I respectfully request that those members of my crew who live in other parts of the country be allowed to visit them with priority transportation orders."

"Request denied," Gorshkov answered tersely.

Borodine flushed. He felt as if he had been severely reprimanded.

"For now," Gorshkov said, "I have nothing more to say to you."

Borodine stood up.

"I will see you at the hearings," Gorshkov said, getting to his feet. "And remember, Comrade Admiral, to send your condolence messages." He reached across the desk and offered his hand.

"I will remember," Borodine answered, shaking Gorshkov's hand.

"Igor, are you all right?" Tanya asked, switching on the lamp on the night table.

Borodine turned from the window. "I couldn't sleep," he said. "It's not easy to sleep in a bed after —"

She patted the empty place next to her. "Come," she said. "I want to be close to you."

Borodine returned to bed.

"Is there something I should know?" Tanya asked, when the room was again in darkness and her arm over Borodine's chest.

Turning toward her, he drew her close and kissed her on the lips. "I love you, Tanya," he said softly.

"I love you too," she answered.

"I'm glad you're here… I mean that you were here for me to come back to."

"Was the mission difficult?" Tanya asked.

Borodine didn't answer. He was sure the apartment was bugged.

Tanya repeated the question.

Borodine shook his head and whispered, "I will tell you another time."

For several moments, Tanya was quiet; then suddenly she bolted up and almost shouted, "You don't mean —"

Borodine clapped his hand over her mouth. "Easy… Easy," he told her.

"You mean they heard everything while we made love?" she asked.

"Yes. They listen, but it means nothing to them."

"But it means something to me," she said.

Borodine caressed the back of her head.

"The KGB?"

"Yes."

"But why?"

"Tanya, it's the way it is," Borodine said.

"But they don't do that with ordinary people."

"I'm not just an ordinary person," he answered, "though sometime I wish I was."

"Did something very bad happen on the mission?" she asked in a whisper.

Borodine hadn't told her anything about the hearings. He didn't want to worry her and he didn't want to spoil his first night home. "The mission," he whispered, "was a disaster."

"But —"

Again he put his hand over her mouth. "Don't ask me any questions," he said. "Tomorrow we will go for a walk and I will tell you what you want to know."

"Just tell me if you're in any danger?" she asked.

For several moments, Borodine considered how he should answer; then he said, "This time I think I might be."

"Oh my darling!" Tanya exclaimed, clinging fiercely to him. "If anything should happen to you —"

"You'll return to my parents with our child," Borodine said sternly. "But nothing will happen to me."

"Hold me!"

Borodine put his arms around her.

"Igor, you're not sorry that you married me?" she asked.

"No, Tanya… No," he answered. "I love you."

"Soon I'll be too big for us to make love."

"Tanya," he said, caressing her stomach, "it is as much my bigness as yours. You carry it, true. But I put it there."

"Let's give the KGB something to really listen to," she said.

Borodine laughed and slipping the nightgown off her shoulders he began to kiss her.

# CHAPTER 6

Earlier in the day, Boxer had spent several hours at Naval Headquarters, where he taped his preliminary statement about the accident. But now he was in an inflatable with Stark at the outboard and he and DB sitting on the gunwale, waiting for the motor to be cut and the craft to lose headway.

Suddenly the throb of the engine stopped and it was silent except for the sound of the lapping water and the cries of two wheeling gulls.

"Good luck," Stark said.

"Go straight back to shore," Boxer responded. "I don't want anyone to get the idea that something is going on out here."

Stark nodded.

Boxer looked at DB. "Ready?" he asked.

"Ready, Skipper," DB answered.

"Go!" Boxer said. He fitted the breathing mask over his face and, armed with an oxygen-fired rifle, he went over the side of the skiff.

DB was down a half a fathom in front of him. His thin, tall frame was already beginning to arch up.

"Stand by," Boxer said, adjusting his radio for short range transmission.

"Standing by, Skipper," DB answered, already head up.

Boxer came down alongside of him. "You hang between five-zero and seven-five feet. I'll go down and have a look."

"Aye, aye, Skipper," DB said and added, "not much visibility."

"Can't ask for everything," Boxer responded and went into a dive. He checked his watch. There was forty minutes left before sunset, but because there was a heavy overcast, his dive time would be cut by a minimum of ten minutes. He keyed DB. "Clear?" he asked.

"Clear, Skipper," DB answered.

Boxer checked his wrist depth gauge. He was down sixty feet. He looked up. DB was following him. He switched channels. "Admiral, radio check one," he said.

"Roger that," Stark said. "Light fog coming in."

"Ten-four," Boxer answered. Then he heard DB call in and Stark answer.

Stark keyed Boxer. "The fog is coming in faster. You might have to abort."

"Ten-four," Boxer answered. "Negative on abort. This is the only chance I'll have. Reaching bottom."

"Roger that," Stark said.

Boxer switched on a high intensity lamp and played it over the bottom. Several crabs scurried out of the beam's way. He keyed Stark. "The bottom's clean."

"Check in at one-hundred yard radius," Stark said.

"Ten-four," Boxer said, beginning a detailed search of the bottom. "Two huge rocks at three-five degrees," he said.

"They're on the chart," Stark answered.

"Nothing east... Moving west."

DB keyed Boxer. "Skipper, there's something moving at about six-zero degrees."

Boxer cut his light and looked up. He couldn't see anything. He keyed Stark. "Anything on the surface?"

"Negative. Abort dive."

"Stand by," Boxer said. "I need photographs."

DB keyed Boxer. "Skipper, two lights closing fast."

"Dive!" Boxer ordered.

"Aye, aye, Skipper," DB said.

Boxer keyed Stark. "Get the hell out of here."

"Negative," Stark answered. "There's a motorboat about three hundred yards off shore. Two of them."

Boxer looked up. The lights came from two battery operated underwater mules.

Suddenly DB was fixed in their twin beams!

Boxer launched himself up toward the lights.

DB broke free from the shafts of light.

Boxer keyed him. "Move toward the shore," he said. "Coming up toward you."

"Aye, aye, Skipper," DB answered.

Boxer moved quickly through the water. The lights were sweeping the water.

DB keyed Boxer. "Skipper, there are three bogies moving at seven-five degrees. Can't shake them."

Boxer was some three dozen yards behind and forty feet below DB. The three men were closing fast. Boxer switched on his light and pointed it at them.

They stopped and one turned and came after him.

Just as Boxer cut his light, the lights from the sea mules caught him. He keyed Stark. "Condition red," he said. "Condition red."

"Roger that," Stark answered.

Boxer slipped the undersea rifle from his shoulder and fired two bursts from the hip. One of the lights went out and the other sea mule suddenly swung off to the right.

The man coming toward him stopped.

Boxer fired again.

The man clutched his leg and started for the surface.

Boxer looked up at DB just as he was caught between the two other divers.

A moment later DB's limp body hung suspended in the water.

The two divers turned toward Boxer.

"Mistake," Boxer growled. He waited until they were no more than fifteen yards from him before he opened fire. The first burst caught one of them in the stomach and the second burst tore away the other's right shoulder. Boxer swam toward DB. A knife was stuck into the young man's chest. He grabbed hold of DB and started for the surface.

A sudden explosion flung him down, breaking his grip on DB. He looked up. Chunks of wreckage drifted slowly down. He pointed his camera at them and took a half a dozen rapid sequence photographs. Then Boxer went after DB's body and holding it close to him, he swam toward the surface.

Boxer, Stark and the local police chief, George Hampton, were standing alongside the police car, whose flashing lights alternately washed their faces red and yellow.

Hampton was a tall, thin man with very large hands. His high cheekbones and black eyes indicated Native American heritage. He leaned against the radio car and asked, "What were you doin' here?" He spoke slowly and with the accent peculiar to the Bay area.

"I already told you," Boxer said. "Scuba diving."

"Admiral, maybe if this was summer I'd half believe you," Hampton said. But it's the middle of November and it's plain miserable out here. Now tell me how that kid was knifed."

"His name is Donald Butts," Boxer said. "Chief Petty Officer Donald Butts. He's a member of the *Barracuda*'s crew."

"Admiral," Hampton said, "if I hadn't seen you on TV last night, or your picture in this morning's paper, I wouldn't know who the hell you were."

"Where have you taken the body?" Stark asked.

"To the hospital morgue, where an autopsy will be done," Hampton said.

"Better notify the Navy before you do anything," Stark told him.

"Goin' to have to notify the Navy about you, Admiral," Hampton said.

"I'm retired," Stark answered.

"But he ain't," Hampton said, looking at Boxer. He shook his head. "This place sure is lively. Last night your ship gets whomped and now you come up with a member of your crew dead."

Boxer sucked in his breath and slowly let it out. He looked at Stark, nodded and said, "We came out here to look for debris."

"Debris?"

"Resulting from the accident," Boxer said. "We were attacked by three men."

"Where are they?"

Boxer pointed to the bay. "Out there. At least one of them might turn up in a few days."

"Dead?"

"Dead."

"You kill him?"

Boxer nodded. "He was coming at me. I didn't have any choice."

"I know the feeling," Hampton commented.

"Listen," Boxer said, "I know this all sounds weird to you. But I can't tell you why we were out here. At least not yet."

"And you just want me to buy that?"

"It was an undercover operation," Boxer said in desperation.

"Com'on Admiral, get off it!"

"Better tell him," Stark said.

Again Boxer took a deep breath and slowly exhaled before he said, "The *Barracuda* was struck by surface-to-surface missiles. Two of them were fired from a high-speed motorboat."

"If you know that, why were you looking for wreckage?" Hampton asked.

"Because I didn't know it for certain. I guessed that was what happened. And now I have photos to prove it. A motorboat was blown up about an hour ago to provide the wreckage for the Navy divers who'll be here tomorrow morning."

"Who fired the missiles?" Hampton asked. "The Russians?"

Boxer shrugged. "I don't know who fired them."

"You have pictures of the wreckage coming down?" Hampton asked; then turning toward the water, he said, "I wonder what kind of fool is out there in this fog."

"Sounds close by," Stark commented.

"I got six good shots," Boxer said, touching the camera.

"Even if I believed you, how could I explain the body?" he asked. "There's no way I can cover that up."

"Don't," Boxer said. "Tell them the body was reported by an unidentified person. You're the only one who knows anything about it. You and the two guys in the ambulance."

"And you can tell them that we came ashore after you arrived on the scene," Stark said.

"They might not buy it," Hampton responded.

"Listen, whoever tried to kill us down there will make another try to get me," Boxer said. "I need some time. If my name or Admiral Stark's is kept out of the newspapers and off TV for a few days, I might have a chance to find the bastard who fired those missiles and who killed DB."

"You're asking me to cover up a murder," Hampton said.

"Just half a cover," Boxer said. "Just keep our names out of it."

"Before I say anything now," Hampton answered, "I want to see what you have on film."

"You have a deal," Boxer told him; then turning to Stark, he said, "I'll be back in less than an hour. When is the helicopter due?"

"About twenty minutes," Stark said, looking at his watch.

"You go back and tell Francine I'll be home later," Boxer said; then looking at Hampton, he asked, "Will I be able to rent a car around here?"

Suddenly Hampton said, "Don't move." He eased into the car and switched off the lights. "We've got company. Get down and go round to bay side."

The three of them hunkered down and crawled to the other side of the vehicle.

"Is that rifle of yours any good?" Hampton asked, slipping his .375 out of its holster.

"It's good," Boxer said, moving the tab from SUB to AIR.

Hampton eased the door open, climbed into the seat and took a handful of rounds from an old metal ammo box and backing out of the car, he gave the rounds to Stark. "Load and lock," he said.

Stark broke the gun, put a round in the chamber of each barrel and quietly closed the gun.

"Are they still there?" Boxer asked.

Hampton nodded. "Back of the trees some," he said.

"How many?"

"A couple, I suspect."

"This isn't the kind of activity recommended for senior citizens," Stark commented dryly.

"Or anyone else," Boxer responded.

Hampton said, "One of you cover the right, the other take the left. I'll watch the front."

Boxer moved to the right and Stark eased around to the left.

"We could be here all night," Hampton whispered.

"Not likely," Boxer answered.

The three of them fell quiet and waited.

Boxer desperately wanted to be home with Francine. Recording the statement was terribly hard, but at the end of the session he was tired and then he had to come out here. He pursed his lips. DB was —

"On the left!" Hampton exclaimed.

"Left!" Stark echoed and squeezed both triggers.

Suddenly four shots exploded from the other side.

Boxer fired a burst.

Hampton spun around and got three rounds off.

"Any chance of someone hearing those shots?" Stark asked, drawing his arm across his forehead to wipe away the sweat.

"Too far away from anyone, or anything," Hampton answered.

"You still want to see those pictures?" Boxer asked.

"Don't have to. Those jokers out there had better have a real good story when I get hold of them, to explain —"

"In the water!" Boxer shouted, whirling around and firing at two figures.

The burst threw one backward and dropped the other face down.

"Christ!" Hampton swore. "How many more are there?"

Boxer waded out and pulled the two dead men up on the beach. Each had used a snorkel to make his way underwater.

"Know them?" Hampton asked.

"Never saw them before," Boxer answered.

"If you don't want a mess of paperwork," Stark said, "take my advice and shove them back in the water. The tide will move them further up the bay."

"You won't be able to explain the kind of slugs the coroner will find in them. They're special."

"I'll decide that later," Hampton said. "Right now we'd better start thinking about that helicopter that's coming in. These bastards mean business and they won't hesitate to try and shoot it down."

"You can bet they'll try," Stark commented.

"You don't happen to have a radio? Something like a CB with you?"

"Negative," Boxer said.

"How the hell were you going to bring that helicopter in?"

"With that," Boxer said, pointing to the high intensity lamp and realizing that it couldn't be used.

"Should have brought a radio," Stark growled. "Just didn't think of it."

"I can get the pilot on car radio," Hampton said. "That's if the people out there don't see me and shoot the hell out of me. And maybe I can get some help —"

"You don't want to bring more people out here," Boxer said.

"Yeah, I forgot that you want half a lid on this. Okay, I'm going to open the door and try to get to the radio. Here goes nothing."

The door swung open and Hampton pushed his body in.

"His call letters are N-five-two-four," Stark said.

Within moments Hampton was on the air, trying to raise the helicopter's pilot.

"This is N-five-two-four," came out of the speaker.

"This is Police Chief George Hampton of Crayville. Do not attempt to pick up your passengers. Heavy fog conditions will make it very dangerous."

"Ten-four," the pilot answered.

Hampton switched off the radio and started to slide out of the car.

"Stay there," Boxer said.

"What?"

"I'm not going to sit here all fucking night. Let's get the hell out of here."

"How?"

"Slide over. Admiral, climb in the rear," Boxer said.

"We're going to be sitting ducks," Hampton commented.

Boxer took the wheel. "Keys?" he asked.

Hampton handed them to him.

"Roll down your window," Boxer said.

"Okay, it's down."

"Now have you got any tear gas cannisters?" Boxer asked.

"Yeah, in a metal box under the seat where the admiral is sitting," Hampton answered.

"What else have you got?"

"A couple of pull-tab magnesium flares."

"You take the tear gas. Admiral, take the flares. As soon as we start to roll, the two of you let as many cannisters and flares fly as you can. I'm going to hold the wheel with one hand and fire as many bursts as I can with the other."

"And you expect us to get out of here alive?" Hampton asked.

"You have a better idea?" Boxer challenged.

"Looks mighty thin to me too," Stark said.

"The reason why we have this Mexican standoff is that they don't have enough men to finish the job. But that doesn't mean they're not going to get reinforcements. Once that happens we're dead."

"Yeah, you got a point there," Hampton admitted.

"Okay, let's move," Boxer said. He eased his rifle out of the window and held it alongside the car. "Now!" he exclaimed, turning on the ignition and flooring the accelerator. The vehicle shot forward. Boxer whipped the wheel over to the right and fired two short bursts.

"Two away!" Hampton shouted.

A flare exploded into dazzling white light behind them.

Two slugs slammed into the rear of the car.

Boxer pulled the wheel to the left; then to the right. They zigzagged along the narrow road, breaking branches on either side of it. "Isn't there a fucking bend in the road?" he yelled.

"Straight for another mile or so," Hampton answered.

The rear window fell apart.

"They're running after us," Stark said.

"Use the shotgun," Boxer told him.

Stark pulled off two rounds.

The sound of the two shots filled the car.

"They stopped," Stark said.

Boxer pulled his rifle back into the car and handing it back to Stark, he said, "I think we made it."

Hampton reached over and switched on the headlights. "It's too dangerous to drive in this kind of fog without having your lights on," he said.

For several moments there was silence in the car; then the three of them guffawed.

"That son-of-a-bitch has more than nine fucking lives," Bruno Morell growled. He was seated at a table across from Tysin in a small, roadside cocktail lounge outside of Fairfax, Virginia.

"Are you sure he was there?" Tysin asked.

"I spent enough time with him aboard the *Turtle* to be able to recognize his voice. Besides, who else would have the balls to shoot their way out of that kind of a situation?"

"And you're sure he was diving?" Tysin questioned.

"What the fuck else would he be doing?"

Tysin picked up some peanuts from a shallow dish in the center of the table. "You know what that means, don't you?"

Morell nodded. "But the divers are going to find debris there when they go down tomorrow morning."

Tysin shook his head. "Boxer is even more dangerous than he was before."

"He killed two of my men and shot up the third so badly, he'll be lucky if he still has his right arm," Morell said. "But we got one of the men with him."

"Got him?" Tysin asked. "What do you mean got him?"

"Put a knife in him," Morell answered.

"What did you do with the body?"

"I don't have the body."

"Does Boxer have the body?"

Morell shrugged. He was a heavyset man with a bull neck. "I don't know … probably."

"What does that mean?"

"There was an ambulance —"

"Then the man was alive?"

"Dead. Believe me he was dead."

"Then the body is in the morgue?"

"Yeah, that's where it probably is," Morell answered, reaching for a handful of peanuts.

Tysin bit his lower lip; then he said, "My guess is that Boxer probably had a member of his crew with him."

"There was a third person."

Tysin's eyebrows went up.

"I don't know who he was," Morell said.

"Boxer, a policeman and an unknown third man and all of them got away," Tysin said sarcastically.

"Listen," Morell said, "you never said anything about Boxer knowing —"

Tysin held up his hand. "I underestimated him."

"That's a dumb thing to do," Morell said.

"Believe me, I won't make that mistake again," Tysin responded.

Morell finished his Dewars on the rocks and looking around for the waitress, he said, "The divers will find the wreckage and you should be able to do the rest."

"He's got to be destroyed," Tysin said. "But maybe we're making a mistake by trying to kill him. Maybe we should try to do it a different way."

"You'll do it if you can get a court-martial to convict him," Morell said.

"Maybe," Tysin said. "But I want something in addition to that. I want him crippled psychologically. I want him hurt so badly that he'll be an emotional wreck."

Morell caught the waitress's attention. "Do you want another drink?" he asked Tysin.

Tysin shook his head. "We're having some friends over for dinner," he said.

"Another of the same," Morell told the waitress when she came to the table; then to Tysin he said, "Yeah, I know what you mean."

"Is that all you can say?"

"Listen," Morell said, "Boxer tried to kill me. No one wants to see him dead — Wait a minute, I think I know someone.

Someone you know too… Sanchez… Sanchez is the man you should speak to. He's got a score to settle with him too."

"No need to say more," Tysin said. "I'll speak to Sanchez. I want you to take a trip out to Crayville and find out who's in the morgue and then I want you to try to find out who was the other man with Boxer."

"I'll go first thing in the morning. Where will I be able to reach you tomorrow evening?"

Tysin was about to tell Morell to call him at home; then he remembered that he would be with Lori. "I'll phone you at the usual number," he said.

"I won't be there until after nine, maybe ten."

"I'll phone you there," Tysin told him.

The waitress returned to the table with Morell's drink.

"I must go now," Tysin said.

Morell nodded. "I might as well stay and have dinner here," he answered.

Tysin stood up. "Ten enough to cover my drinks?" he asked, going for his wallet.

"Next time it's your treat," Morell said.

"Thanks," Tysin responded.

Morell raised his glass. "Luck and good health," he toasted.

"Luck and good health," Tysin repeated; then he left the table and walked to the cloak room. That Boxer had gone down to look for the wreckage of the speedboat didn't sit well with him at all.


Boxer sat in the large easy chair on the side of the fireplace and Stark occupied a club chair on the other side. Francine paced back and forth between the two men and the fireplace.

"I'm having difficulty understanding all of this," Francine said, suddenly stopping.

Neither Boxer or Stark made any effort to speak.

"Who would be so anxious to kill you, Jack, that they'd be willing to kill so many other men to get at you?"

Boxer shrugged. But he didn't answer her.

"More to the point, why would they want to kill you?"

"It could be the Russians," Stark said.

"Could be," Boxer answered. "But I don't think so."

"Then who do you think it could be?" Francine pressed. "I want to know who you think it could be?"

"I don't really know," Boxer answered.

"What are you going to do about DB?"

"He can't do anything," Stark said. "He can't even claim his body until his identity is established. And then the Navy has priority."

Francine shook her head. "I can't believe these things have happened," she said in a low voice.

Boxer stared silently at the flames in the fireplace. He had said nothing about the men he had killed.

"I suggest we go to bed," Stark said. "We're not going to come up with any answers tonight."

"I won't be able to sleep tonight," Francine said. "I'm too keyed up. Besides we have another problem —"

"What other problem?" Boxer asked.

"Your adoption of Chuck was blocked by a court order," she said.

"I don't understand."

"Chuck's aunt and the high school principal De Mattao asked the court to postpone giving you legal custody of the boy until —"

Boxer launched himself out of the chair. "That son-of-a-bitch put her up to it. She hasn't got the brains to come up with it on her own. Now what the hell is going to happen?"

"You're going to have to prove you're not guilty of moral turpitude."

"What the hell does that mean?"

"That you're sufficiently moral to raise Chuck."

Boxer went to the fireplace and leaned on the mantel. "And how do I do that?"

"You'll have to go before a judge."

"Another hearing?"

Francine nodded. "Yes, another hearing. The decision will lie with the judge, at least as far as legally adopting him. Since he's over sixteen, he can choose to live with you. But you will not be his legal father."

"I want him to know I care enough about him to be his legal father," Boxer said.

"Then you must appear in court."

"When?"

"A month from tomorrow," Francine said.

Boxer took a deep breath and slowly exhaled. "Tomorrow we'll fly up to New York and see Chuck."

"He called here today."

"Does he know about the court order?" Boxer asked.

"Yes. He's very concerned about you. He asked me over and over again if you're all right. I tried to assure him you were, but I didn't think he really believed me."

"We'll go to New York tomorrow," Boxer said. "I want to see Chuck and John."

"Are you sure you want me with you?" Francine asked.

"I want you with me," he answered; then to Stark, he said, "Admiral, would you use some of your connections to find out what Mason and Tysin know or don't know?"

"Yes," Stark said, pulling himself out of the club chair. "Good night."

"Good night," Boxer and Francine answered in unison.

"See you some time tomorrow," Stark said, as he mounted the steps.

Boxer waited until Stark was out of earshot before he said, "He's had a hard time. It was touch and go for quite a while out there."

Francine moved closer to Boxer and put her arms around him. "I was frightened out of my mind until you walked in."

Boxer held her tightly.

"Jack, you don't think it's the Russians, do you?"

He shook his head. "Maybe some other foreign group, but not the Russians. Don't ask me why I think that because I won't be able to give you an answer, other than it's just a gut feeling."

"Let's go up to bed," Francine said, nuzzling his ear. "I want you to make love to me."

Boxer put his arm around her shoulders and said, "The best I'll be able to do tonight is hold you."

"That bad out there?" she questioned.

"We almost didn't make it back."

"Would you mind if I tried some of my magic on you?"

"Try anything you want," Boxer said, leading her toward the stairs. "Whatever you do, I'm sure the pleasure will be mine."

Dressed in a white jumpsuit and a black leather jacket, Lori-Ann sat behind the wheel of her white Trans-Am. The windshield wipers moved back and forth, preventing the light rain from blurring her vision. The glow from the dashboard gave her face a green pallor. The radio was tuned to a local rock station and her body moved to the beat of the music. Even though it was two o'clock in the morning and the streets were deserted, she drove slowly. When she came to the parking area in front of the Lincoln Memorial, she eased into a diagonal parking slot and shifted into neutral. She left the engine running, but she lowered the volume of the radio. She placed her white leather handbag on the console next to her and opened it wide enough for her to reach a high-powered .22 revolver should the need arise.

Her body still moving to the beat of the music, Lori-Ann took a cigarette from the open pack in the tray on the dash and lit it. She didn't like meetings in the middle of the night and she especially didn't like them when she was going to meet the person for the first time.

She had her last control for almost five years and had grown used to his ways and his sexual needs, though he really didn't have too many. He was almost seventy. Now and then he enjoyed having her sleep next to him, but seldom could he manage an erection and even less frequently could he have an orgasm. Except for the few interludes when he wanted her in bed, their relationship was almost like that of father and daughter. They were concerned about each other's well being and he worried over the kind of men she dated. Several times they even went on vacation together to places like Paris, Rome, Mexico and this last summer, to Cape Cod.

Lori-Ann blew smoke against the windshield, pressed a button on the side of the door and the window next to her moved down. She looked at the clock in the dashboard. It was two-fifteen. She checked it against her watch. The time was the same. She was about to say *late*, when suddenly she saw a man walk down the steps and come toward the car.

He was tall, thin and he either needed a shave or was following the latest fashion for men and allowing stubble to decorate his jaw. He wore a tweed jacket, woolen scarf around his neck and a wide-brimmed leather hat. He came directly up to the car, bent down to look at her and in Russian, he said, "Open the door on the other side."

She nodded. He had a deep resonant voice and his face was craggy. She guessed he was probably in his late thirties, or early forties.

"Drive," he said, speaking in English.

"Where?"

"I don't care where… Just drive."

Lori-Ann shifted into reverse, backed out of the parking slot, shifted into drive and eased her foot down on the accelerator. She decided to circle the city on the Beltway.

"My name," he said, still speaking in English, "is Daniel Frumkin."

She gave him a quick glance.

"No cracks about it," he said. "Since the choice wasn't mine to make, the comments aren't yours to make."

Lori-Ann remained silent. But she didn't like his tone, or what he said.

"You will report to me with the same frequency that you reported to your other control," Frumkin told her.

"Where?" she asked.

"You will call this number three times a day," he said, handing her a slip of paper with a seven-digit number on it. "Memorize it and destroy the paper."

"Yes master," she said. The words were out before she could stop them.

"That's not funny," he responded. "Not funny at all."

Lori-Ann suppressed a smile.

"Your former control told me that you have been able to achieve an extremely sensitive position," Frumkin said.

"If you mean that I am Mister Tysin's private secretary, the answer is yes," Lori-Ann responded. She wasn't going to tell him about the change in the relationship that had occurred on the floor of Tysin's office the previous morning, or about the special assignment he had given her until she knew more about him.

"There is no change in your assignment," he said. "You are to apprise me of whatever sensitive issues pass through your hands."

Lori-Ann nodded. She noticed that Frumkin had repositioned himself since he'd entered the car and was now sitting catty-corner, appraising her. Again, she suppressed a smile. With a seemingly natural gesture, she removed her right hand from the wheel, touched her hair and then placed it in the V at the top of the jumpsuit's zipper, forcing it down until she was sure a portion of her breasts would be visible whenever she turned slightly toward him.

"Have you anything special to report?" Frumkin asked.

To protect herself, she answered, "There appears to be some real concern about Admiral Boxer on Tysin's part."

"How does this 'real concern,' as you put it, show itself?"

"Mister Tysin —"

"Part of your assignment was to establish a sexual relationship with Mister Tysin and according to your former control, you were sure that such a relationship would develop in the immediate future."

"It will," Lori-Ann answered; then she added, "Comrade Frumkin, I am well acquainted with the requirements of my assignment."

"Tell me more about Mister Tysin's concern about Admiral Boxer," he said.

Lori-Ann was furious about the way he ignored her comment. "We'll be coming back to where we came on the highway," she said. "There are police cars on the Beltway and one of them just might wonder why a car is —"

"Take the next exit off that will lead us into Virginia," Frumkin said. "Then drive to Falls Church. Do you know how to get there?"

Lori-Ann nodded. "Why are we going there?"

Frumkin shrugged. "You wanted to drive somewhere. That's as good as any place."

"What I really want to do is go to sleep," she said.

"All right, go off the highway and drive to the Capitol. I'll leave you there. But first I want more information on Tysin's concern about Admiral Boxer."

"He just happened to be on the phone when I walked into the office," she lied, "and I heard him say, 'I'm very concerned about Admiral Boxer'."

"Were those his exact words?"

"Close to them," Lori-Ann answered, moving on to an exit ramp.

"Did he refer to him by his rank and his name, or just by his name?" Frumkin asked.

Suddenly she sensed danger. Beads of sweat broke out on her forehead. She knew she had to come up with a plausible answer, or risk whatever consequences he'd give. She steadied her voice and said, "Usually he doesn't include his rank, but during that phone conversation he did."

Frumkin said nothing.

Lori-Ann glanced at him.

He smiled at her.

She looked at the roadway ahead of her, saw the light turn red and slammed her foot down on the brake. The car stopped just as another sports car flashed across the street. Lori-Ann's heart skipped a beat and began to race. She was sorry now that she had decided to play a game with him. But she had no choice but to continue, at least for the remainder of this meeting.

"Your light," Frumkin told her.

"Yes, my light," she said and moved her foot from the brake to the accelerator.

"Go to your apartment," Frumkin told her.

She was about to ask *why*, but decided to remain silent.

"Is your lover there?" Frumkin asked.

"Yes."

"Doesn't he question you —"

"I don't question him and he doesn't question me," she said. "We enjoy having sex with one another, but neither of us wants to be restricted to the other."

"A thoroughly modern relationship," Frumkin commented.

There was an unmistakable tone of sarcasm in his voice that made her look at him and say, "It suits our purpose, doesn't it?"

"Do you think you can turn him?"

Lori-Ann stopped for another red light. "I never considered it," she said. "But my first reaction would be to say no. He comes from a wealthy family and his politics are conservative."

"And you pretend that yours are too?"

"Yes," she answered.

"How long have you been living with Mister Ronald Baxter, the third?"

"It will be two years at the end of the month," Lori-Ann said.

"How many times a week do you have sex with him?" Frumkin asked matter-of-factly.

"Wait a minute —"

"Answer the question," Frumkin snapped.

"Once, maybe twice."

"How many times?" Frumkin demanded.

The light changed and Lori-Ann's foot went down hard on the accelerator, harder than she intended. The tires squealed on the wet street surface and the rear of the car fishtailed. "I'm sorry," she said, bringing the vehicle under control. "I didn't mean to do that."

"How many times?" Frumkin asked again, his voice harder than before.

"Sometimes once every ten to fourteen days. Sometimes, once a month. What has this to do with my assignment?"

"You share the same bed with Mister Baxter?"

She nodded.

"Did you ever discuss his lack of interest?" Frumkin asked.

"Yes, we talked about it," Lori-Ann said. "Ron works very hard. He —"

"He has another lover," Frumkin said.

"What did you say?" She started to veer toward the curb.

"Don't stop," he told her and then he repeated what he had said.

"I don't believe you," Lori-Ann responded.

"There's no need for you to be jealous. It's not another woman. If you can find comfort in it, you're the only woman in his life."

She flicked her eyes toward him. "I have to stop just for a couple of minutes. Please."

Frumkin nodded.

Lori-Ann eased the car over to the curb and brought it to a halt. "Tell me how you found this out?"

"Your former control told me."

"He knew?"

"For a year," Frumkin said. "He didn't tell you because he did not want to disturb the relationship. I don't want to disturb it either. But I would be more comfortable with it if Ron would cooperate with us. If not for deeply felt political and sociological reasons, then to protect his position in the Justice Department, to say nothing of his position in the Baxter family. Did you know that when his father dies, he will come into the Baxter fortune, which is estimated at twenty-seven million dollars."

Lori-Ann gasped. "I had no idea his family had that kind of fortune."

"They do and it's growing every hour of every day," Frumkin said.

Lori-Ann reached for a cigarette, but her hand was trembling so violently, she wasn't able to align the flame from the lighter with the tip of the cigarette.

"Let me help you," Frumkin offered, taking the lighter from her and holding it until the cigarette was lit. Then he said, "I have a plan that might be beneficial to you, me, Ron and most importantly to our government."

Lori-Ann let the smoke out of her nose and mouth. She needed a drink to steady her.

"Simply," Frumkin went on, "you marry him. Once that's done, he has the perfect cover. You have the perfect cover and I have two operators, who move in very high circles and are very, very wealthy."

"Three minor details," she said. "He hasn't asked me. He hasn't been turned, and his father hasn't died."

"One at a time, my dear. One at a time. Depending on circumstances, his father can soon be dead. That is a very simple matter to arrange. The marriage and the turning are in your hands."

She stubbed out her cigarette.

Frumkin took hold of her hand. "Ron has aspirations that go far beyond the Justice Department. He would be a very valuable person for us to have on the inside."

Lori-Ann nodded.

"You seem to be upset by all this," Frumkin said, freeing her hand.

"I just wasn't prepared to have so much happening the first time we met," she answered.

He reached over, took hold of the zipper tab and slowly pulling it down, he said, "You do have exquisite breasts." And he placed his hand across them. "Is the rest of you as beautiful?"

Lori-Ann sucked in her breath and slowly exhaling, she answered, "That judgment has to be yours."

"Yes, it will be. But not tonight. Tonight you have too many other things to think about." And he pulled the zipper up. "I'll leave you here," he said, smiling; then he opened the door and left the car.

A moment later, Lori-Ann was alone. "Bastard," she swore out loud, "fucking bastard!" She threw the shift into drive, gunned the engine and burned rubber as she raced away.

# CHAPTER 7

Jay Corless Archer and William White were breakfasting with the President in the small dining room of the White House.

Jay, as he was familiarly called by his friends, was tall, gray-haired and had a booming laugh, while Billy was somewhat shorter than his friend and though also gray, had his hair dyed brown, which made him look years younger than Jay, or the President, even though he was pushing sixty-five. Both men wore hand-tailored suits and hand-made leather boots. By comparison to Jay and Billy, the President, who was not as tall and was suffering from a cold, lacked the commanding presence of either of the other men.

"Mister President," Jay asked, spearing a piece of sausage with his fork, "have you spoken to Boxer?"

"Other than to use his name in my official statement of condolence to him and the families of the men who were killed, I have not spoken to, or about him to anyone."

"Sad," Billy said. "Very sad."

"Yes," the President acknowledged. "But this may give Tysin and Mason the opportunity to slap his wrists."

Jay smiled. "And through them do some wrist slapping yourself, eh?"

"You have to admit, I had to eat crow when he suggested that we give a medal to that Russian admiral," the President said.

"Kind of caught everyone with their pants down," Billy commented.

"That's for sure," the President said. "And I tell you it was fucking embarrassing."

"I believe it," Jay said, taking a sip of coffee. He and Billy had known the President for over twenty-five years and it was their money that helped get him elected to Congress from their district in south-west Texas. The President, whose name was Richard Spooner, was born and raised in New York. His father, Troy Spooner, was a very imaginative tax attorney, with whom Jay had business dealings in the early fifties, before the man died of cardiac arrest.

"But I didn't ask you to breakfast to discuss Boxer," the President said.

"Didn't think you did," Billy responded. "This is too early for us to get up. I feel like I just went to sleep."

"You just about did," Jay laughed. "We had a wonderful time last evenin'."

"It's a hell of a lot easier to do that with the wives back in Texas," Billy said. "There were a few women at the party last night who —" He felt Jay kick him under the table.

"Why did you have us to breakfast, other than you just happen to like our company?"

"A huge deposit of oil and natural gas has been discovered off Antarctica by an International Geophysical Expedition and that means the Russians know as much about it as we do."

"How large are the estimates?" Jay asked.

"Twice as large as the North Slope," the President answered.

Billy made a low whistling sound; then said, "That's not just large, that's humongous."

"Can you raise enough capital to develop it?" the President asked.

"How much would be enough?" Billy questioned.

"My experts say two billion just to start," the President said.

Again Billy gave a low whistle.

"We might have to work a mite harder than we're used to doing," Jay said. "But we can raise the money."

"It'll be split sixteen ways from Sunday," Billy added.

The President nodded; then he said, "After I finish my term, I'd like very much to be the chief counsel for a large corporation. I've given the matter a great deal of thought and that kind of position would give the kind of lifestyle I and my family would like."

Jay stirred sugar into his coffee. "I don't think there'd be any difficulty with that."

"No difficulty at all," Billy seconded.

"But when there's something as big as Antarctica involved, there's got to be some difficulty," the President said with a smile.

"I was wondering when the other shoe was going to fall," Billy said.

"The Russians know about this too," the President said, "and now we've got to know what they're going to do."

"Can't you find that out through your usual sources?" Jay asked.

The President shook his head. "They suddenly made any of the openings we have tighter than a virgin's quim."

"You want us to try through our sources?" Billy questioned.

"I want one or both of you to go there and find out what you can."

"That's a pretty big want, Mister President," Jay said. "You're asking us to be spies."

"Just nose around a bit. The Russians trust you."

"That's just it: they trust us. That trust has taken my daddy and me almost two lifetimes to build and you're asking me to put it at risk. To put some twenty million dollars of investments at risk. That's a lot to risk."

"Not you personally —"

"The fact that it might be traced back to us puts us personally at risk."

"I agree," Billy said.

"That information will be needed before any development can begin," the President responded. "Even before you start raising the capital to develop the field."

"That's true," Jay answered.

"True," Billy echoed.

"Each of you should be worth in the order of a hundred million from this new company, to say nothing of your yearly salaries and other perks that would come your way."

"That's if we're not caught," Jay answered.

"Think on it," the President said.

"You can be sure that we will."

"Before we do too much thinking on it," Billy said, "if we agree to do what you asked, it won't be without some horse tradin' involved."

The President grinned. "I'd have been surprised if there wasn't any."

"Good," Billy said. "As long as you know it."

"You wouldn't just happen to know what you'd be interested in trading, would you?" the President asked. "After all, I wouldn't want to be in the position where a trade couldn't take place."

"For what you're asking us to do, there must be at least a three for one trade," Jay said.

"Even trade," the President said.

Jay shook his head.

The President looked at Billy.

"He does the deal. I just put it on the table."

"Two," the President said.

"Three," Jay answered, cutting the end of a long Cuban cigar with a small gold penknife, then lighting the other end.

After a moment's hesitation, the President asked, "What do you want?"

"That nothing happens to Boxer," Jay said.

"What?"

Billy raised his eyebrows, but remained silent.

"I know that certain people are gunning for him. I want your assurance that nothing will happen to him. But if —"

"Nothing will happen to him," Jay repeated, his voice suddenly becoming hard. "That's part of the deal, or there's no deal."

"Give me the other two parts before I agree to anything," the President said, lifting the coffee cup to his lips.

"To campaign for Boxer when he runs for Congress," Jay said.

The President gagged and began to cough. Tears came to his eyes and it took several moments before he was able to say, "You must be joking."

"And the third part of the deal is you agree in writing to the first two parts," Jay said.

The President flushed. "That shows very little trust," he said.

"That shows just how much I want to protect what I get," Jay answered. "I'll think on what you want and you think on what I want. The next time we have breakfast together we'll give each other our answer."

The President nodded. "What you're asking sticks in my craw."

"You can always say *no deal*; that's your option," Billy said.

"You go along with this?" the President asked.

Billy nodded.

"So you gents think there's politics in the admiral's future!" the President exclaimed.

"I think there might be a chance," Jay answered.

"A chance at all this too?" the President questioned, making a sweeping gesture with his hand.

"A chance, if he wants it bad enough," Billy said.

"Does he have any idea what he has in store for him?" And before either Billy or Jay could answer, the President said, "Let me rephrase that question: does he have any idea what you have in store for him?"

"None," Jay said.

"And you think he'll go for it?"

"Don't know."

"A great many people will take exception to his lifestyle, to say nothing of his friendship with the Russians."

"He's not friendly with the Russians; he's friendly with one Russian," Jay said. "But, as the saying goes, we'll cross that bridge when we come to it. And as far as his lifestyle goes, we're living in the nineteen-nineties. People's attitudes are a lot more liberal about lifestyles than they were even ten years ago."

The President helped himself to another cup of coffee. "When do you expect to broach the subject of his political future to him?" he asked.

"In the not too distant future," Jay answered. "Before I do anything, I need your commitment first."

"I'll give you my answer in a few days," the President said. "But since we've been friends for many, many years, it's only fair to tell you that I think you're making a very serious mistake. Boxer has many powerful enemies. The cost of bringing him into Congress will be more than it's worth. You will never be able to control him. Kinkade couldn't control him."

"Can Tysin?"

"He's hoping the accident will give him the leverage he needs. I left it entirely in his hands."

"If your answer is *yes*," Jay said, "it can't be left that way."

"I'm aware of that," the President answered. "And if I go along with you, when could you leave for Russia?"

"Two to three weeks after we settle everything," Jay said.

"How long do you think it might take you to get a line on what they intend doing?"

Jay shrugged. "What do you think, Billy?"

"A week. A month... Maybe longer. One thing for sure, it's not going to be easy."

"Never thought it would be," the President responded and looking at his watch, he said, "Well gents, I have another meeting in a few minutes."

"Thanks for breakfast," Jay said.

"My pleasure," the President answered. "Give me a call in a few days. Perhaps we'll have cocktails together."

"That'd be nice," Billy responded.

"By the way," Jay said, "the wife and I are throwing a big Christmas shindig and she asked me to invite you and your wife personally. She'll be sending out invitations soon."

"Haven't missed one of your Christmas parties in twenty-five years," the President said, "and I don't intend to miss this one."

"Good!" Jay exclaimed. "Very good!"

Boxer and Francine cabbed it from La Guardia airport to New Dorp High School, where they met with De Mattao, the school's principal and the man, who together with Chuck's aunt, filed an injunction against the proposed adoption.

After the introductions, Boxer got directly to the point. "I want to know how and why you got involved in this?" he asked.

De Mattao smiled. He was a man of middling height, with an underslung jaw, a large moustache and a stomach that hung over his belt. "As the guardian of all these young people, I felt it was my duty to make sure that Charles was —"

"Cut the crap," Boxer flashed. "You couldn't care less about Chuck and I know Ms. Caliendo doesn't care one way or another."

De Mattao flushed. "I'm afraid you misjudged his aunt. She cares very much."

Boxer looked at Francine and nodded. It was a prearranged signal.

"Mister De Mattao," Francine began in a silken smooth voice, "perhaps my client has been too hasty. But I think there must be some room for negotiations."

De Mattao smiled. "For civilized people, there is always room for that," he said.

Boxer watched De Mattao's eyes devour Francine.

"Why don't you tell me what is negotiable and what isn't," Francine said.

"You understand that once Charles leaves Ms. Caliendo, she will lose a certain amount of income. Not that she uses it for herself, but —"

"I certainly understand," Francine said. "Now how much do you think she will lose?"

Again De Mattao smiled. "I'm sure you know the amount."

"We are prepared to continue those payments for a period of five years," Francine said, giving De Mattao the figure that she and Boxer had agreed on during the flight up from Washington.

"I am sure that will please her," De Mattao said.

"Is there anything else?" Francine asked.

Boxer was sure there would be.

"As a matter of fact there is," De Mattao said.

"Your position," Francine told him before he could define it.

De Mattao nodded.

"How much?" Boxer asked.

Francine gave him a *Let me handle it look* and said, "Naturally we understand that you have a role in all of this."

"Suppose we look at fifty thousand," De Mattao said.

Boxer started out of his chair.

Francine shot him a withering glance; then she calmly said, "We were thinking more like ten thousand."

De Mattao leaned back into his chair. "If that's your offer, we have nothing more to discuss."

"Fifteen."

"Twenty-five."

"Twenty-five," Francine echoed.

De Mattao gave them an oily smile. "Naturally I don't want that in a check."

"How do you want it?"

"In an automobile," he said. "Which you will buy in your name, Admiral, and sell to me for a few hundred dollars, which by the way you will give me in cash."

Boxer glared at him, but kept silent.

"That will be fine," Francine said.

De Mattao leaned forward and took a pen out of the onyx pen holder. "I'll write the name of the car and the dealer from whom you will purchase it," he said. "The dealer happens to a very good friend of mine."

"I didn't know you had any," Boxer responded.

"All of us can't save the world, Admiral, or kill as many men as you have. Some of us must make do with whatever chance throws our way."

"And some of us are just jackals," Boxer answered angrily.

"Gentlemen," Francine said, "there's no need for any of that. We've reached an agreement and that solves the problem."

De Mattao pushed the slip of paper across the desk.

"When will you withdraw the injunction?" Francine asked.

"As soon as you leave the office," De Mattao said, "I'll call Judge Lelow and have it withdrawn."

Francine nodded.

"You see, Admiral," De Mattao said, with a broad smile, "you made me eat crow the last time we met and now you have to eat a much bigger bird."

Boxer flushed.

"Let it be," Francine told him.

"My friend is expecting you," De Mattao said. "He knows exactly what I want. All you have to do is sign the papers and write the check."

Nodding, Francine picked up the piece of paper and said, "Oh, by the way, do you happen to know a Howard Kiminsky?"

De Mattao flushed.

"I happen to know you do and rather intimately, from the tapes and photographs I have," Francine said.

"You don't —"

"I certainly do," she said. "I'm sure the Staten Island newspapers would find them very, very interesting."

"But —"

"Of course everything is negotiable," she said.

"I —"

"Why don't you pick up the phone and speak to the judge now, and then while we're still here, phone Ms. Caliendo and tell her that you've changed your mind, or whatever else you call it."

Boxer's jaw almost went slack. Francine had never told him about the tapes or the photographs.

"Call the judge first," Francine said.

While De Mattao picked up the phone, Francine smiled at Boxer and whispered, "While you were away, I thought it would be wise to do a bit of research work on him and I wanted to surprise you with what I found."

"You sure as hell did," Boxer told her. "You sure as hell surprised me."

This was Tysin's fourth meeting in the apartment with Lori. For him, the days couldn't pass too quickly. He had sex with Lori three times and he couldn't think of anything else. She was almost always in his thoughts. Whenever she came into his office, he had to restrain himself from caressing her, from doing the things he had done the first time he had sex with her. He couldn't look at her without having a mental image of her naked. He was falling in love with her and from the way she responded to him, he was sure she was experiencing the same emotion.

Lori came to the door wearing a blue lounging robe with nothing underneath it. She smiled and as soon as he was inside and the door closed, she put her arms around him. "I'm really glad you could get away tonight," she said.

"You smell so good," he whispered.

She took his coat and hat and hung them in the foyer closet. "Does it still look as if it's going to rain?" she asked.

"Yes. A few drops fell just as I walked here from the car," he said, walking deeper into the apartment and looking around. He was amazed at the transformation. Just a few days ago it was nothing more than a couple of rooms with furniture and now it was recognizably a place where a young woman lived. There were reproductions of some various paintings on the walls. He recognized one was of a Van Gogh, another was a Cezanne and Matisse. There were even curtains on the windows.

"You like it?" Lori asked, joining him.

He put his arm around her waist. "It's really charming," he said.

She kissed him on the cheek. "I had lunch with Ms. Johnson," she told him.

"And?"

"Oh, she was only too willing to talk about the admiral. Her sister some years back had a very passionate affair with him."

Tysin let go of her and walked into the combination living and dining room. "Where is the sister now?" he asked, as he started to sit in a rust colored easy chair.

"She was murdered," Lori answered.

Tysin remained standing. His eyes opened wide. "Does she suspect that Boxer —"

Lori shook her head. "No. According to her, Boxer has other problems."

Tysin sat down. "What kind of problems?"

"You ready for this one?"

"Will I need a drink after you tell me?" he asked.

"You might," she answered.

"Then you had better fix me a very, very dry martini," Tysin said.

Lori repeated his request and went to the cupboard above the sink and took out a bottle of gin and one of vermouth.

Tysin enjoyed seeing the way the gown clung to her body when she made certain movements. The thought crossed his mind that even after the Company's need for the apartment passed, he might try to keep it for her. It wouldn't be difficult to bury its cost in the monies used for miscellaneous expense.

Lori returned with two cocktail glasses and handing one to him, she sat down on the arm of the easy chair. "Toast," she said.

"You make one," he answered, looking up at her. The top of the robe was completely open, exposing both her breasts, and because of the way she was sitting, the bottom of the robe was parted to her thigh.

She smiled at him, clinked her glass against his and putting his hand on her bare thigh, Lori said, "To us, may we love for a long, long time."

"I'd like that," he said, before drinking.

"So would I," she whispered.

"Now, tell me what you've discovered," Tysin said.

"It's about the admiral," she said. "He has a problem."

"He has many problems," Tysin answered. "What new one have you discovered?"

"The admiral suffers from what Linda Johnson thinks is claustrophobia."

"You're joking, aren't you?"

Lori shook her head.

"But how could that be?" Tysin asked. "He's a submariner; they're —"

"She doesn't much like him," Lori told him.

Tysin finished his drink. "Is there any more left?"

She nodded. "I'll get it," she said, taking his glass and standing.

Tysin called after her. "How does she know he's claustrophobic?"

"According to her," Lori answered, "they were together during one of his attacks."

"When?"

"Several months ago. Before he and Wheeler became a pair."

"Did she give you any more details?"

"She wanted to do an interview on him," Lori answered. "That was after he and that Russian managed to stop Captain Bush from blowing all of us up."

Tysin stood and began to pace. "If I could prove —"

Lori returned with one glass and handed it to him.

"Aren't you going to have another?" he asked.

She came close to him. "Later, maybe. But you go ahead and drink yours."

Tysin nodded and drank. He needed the drink to steady him. He was on fire emotionally and on fire professionally. "Tell me the rest of what she told you," he said.

"They were in her apartment when it happened," Lori explained. "They had gone there to screw. Linda was very straightforward about that. It seems that she is half-sister to a woman whom Boxer had been seeing and was interested in trying it herself."

"Slow down," Tysin said. "Who's the woman?"

"It doesn't matter. She was murdered several years ago. But Linda is a half-sister."

"Okay, now tell me what happened in the apartment."

"Nothing. They went there to screw, but the admiral started to act strange."

"How strange?"

"Very, according to Linda."

"Details," Tysin said, pacing again. "I need details."

"He started to sweat, turned very white and ran out of the apartment."

"He didn't do anything, then?"

"Nothing."

Tysin stopped, finished his drink and put the empty glass down on an end table. "He ran from the apartment?"

"That's what she said."

"Did she remember what he said?" Tysin asked.

"Only that he was 'sick' and that he was 'sorry'."

Tysin repeated the two words; then he said, "Do you think she'd be willing to testify before the Naval Board of Inquiry?"

Lori shrugged.

"She'd be well paid," Tysin said.

"How well?"

"First find out whether she'd be willing to come before the Board; then try to get some idea what she'd want in return. I'd like her to suggest an amount."

"I'll do my best," Lori answered.

"I'm sure you will," Tysin said, drawing her to him.

Lori tilted her head up, closed her eyes and gave him her lips.

"I called you to my office," Admiral Gorshkov said, looking across the desk at Borodine, "because I wanted to relieve you of any anxiety you might have about your future."

Borodine shifted slightly forward. He had received a telephone call at twenty-three hundred hours the previous night from an officer on the admiral's staff ordering to present himself to the admiral at ten hundred the following morning. No explanation had been given.

"Fate, or chance has come to your rescue," Gorshkov said, "or to put it bluntly, something has occurred that has allowed me to do a bit of horse trading." The admiral smiled. "Didn't know I was an old horse trader, did you? My father and my grandfather were horse traders before the Revolution. I'm the only one in the family who ever went to sea. My four brothers were in the army. All of them were killed in the war against the Nazis." He opened the humidor and taking out a cigar, he gestured to Borodine to take one too. "Comrade Admiral Polyakov wanted to bring you up on charges."

Borodine nodded. "I know that, Comrade Admiral."

Gorshkov blew smoke. "He would have too. The Comrade Premier was ready to go along with him, but something came up. Something as remote as a huge oil field having been discovered in Antarctica."

Borodine lit the cigar and asked, "What does that have to do with me?"

"We want to develop that field," Gorshkov said.

"I still can't even guess at the connection between the oil field and myself," Boxer said.

"Several of my experts think we can control the area if we build a fortress —"

"On land?"

"The field is two hundred miles out at sea," Gorshkov said. "The fortress will have to be built at sea."

"A ship."

"In a matter of speaking," Gorshkov said. "It will be constructed from one of those huge icebergs that break off from the ice cap. In fact it will be exploded off the glacier and then towed a few miles out to sea, where it will be converted into a floating fortress, complete with a small nuclear power plant will be used to keep it from drifting into warm currents.

That iceberg will serve as our base and our first drilling platform. When we bring in the first well, we should have no difficulty claiming the field."

"Comrade Admiral, do I understand that we are going to use an iceberg —"

"The interior will be hollowed out and rebuilt to serve our needs."

"I still don't understand the connection between myself and—"

"You and your *Sea Dragon* will go to the Antarctic to protect Ice Base One until it is capable of protecting itself," Gorshkov said.

"The *Sea Dragon* is in need of repair," Borodine answered.

"She will be totally repaired before you put to sea," Gorshkov told him. "The laser gun is being removed and other modifications are being made that are based on your recommendations and those of your EO."

"Excuse me, Comrade Admiral —"

"Ah yes, the connection between you and the oil field!" Gorshkov exclaimed. "The Premier wants to develop this oil field very badly. He is sure that by developing it, Russia will become the leader in the development of other natural resources in that area of the world. He wanted me to send a squadron of ships to protect Ice Base One, but I convinced him that it could be more effectively done by you in command of the *Sea Dragon* and if you were going to be sent on such an important mission, it would be absurd to allow charges to be brought against you."

"Thank you, Comrade Admiral, for your show of support," Borodine said. "I am deeply grateful."

Gorshkov nodded. "If this scheme hadn't come along," he said, "I doubt if I could have stopped Comrade Admiral Polyakov from bringing charges against you."

"Thank you again," Borodine responded.

"There is one contingency, however, which you must agree to before you are completely safe," Gorshkov said.

Borodine's stomach suddenly knotted. He knew intuitively that it had something to do with Polyakov.

"Comrade Admiral Polyakov will be in overall charge of Ice Base One," Gorshkov said and then, pointing his cigar at Borodine, he added, "and therefore you will be under his direct command again."

Borodine felt alternately hot and cold.

"That is the only condition that the Premier and Polyakov will accept and in return no charges will be brought against you. But if you refuse, the command of the *Sea Dragon* will go to someone else and you will have to answer Polyakov's charges against you."

"Has he agreed to have me under his command again?" Borodine asked.

"He will," Gorshkov said. "He wants to prove that he is more than just a desk admiral."

Borodine leaned back into the chair and took a long drag on the cigar; then letting the smoke rush out of his mouth, he said, "I don't really have much choice if I still want a career in the Navy, do I?"

Gorshkov shook his head. "It was the best deal I could make."

"Do you want my answer now?"

"Yes. I said I would get back to the Premier before twelve hundred."

"I agree," Borodine said in a low voice.

"Very good!" Gorshkov exclaimed.

"But with all due respect," Borodine said, "the man is a fool."

"Yes, he probably is," Gorshkov answered. "But never forget that fools often have friends in very high places."

Borodine didn't answer.

# CHAPTER 8

Mason entered the foyer of the Petite Auberge, a small but very expensive French restaurant just outside Fairfax, Virginia. Tysin was already seated at the bar.

Mason gave his coat and hat to the hat check girl and pocketed the ticket. Before he went to the bar, he paused and looked at Tysin. Though he was facing the other way, Mason could clearly see his reflection in the mirror behind the bar. There was something different about the man, something that he couldn't quite identify. The thought raced through his mind that Tysin might be having an affair but Tysin was too uptight and too cautious a man to indulge himself that way.

"Sorry, I'm a bit late," Mason said, "but getting out of the city tonight took longer than usual."

Tysin nodded. "It gave me some time to think," he said, raising the martini glass to his lips.

Mason settled on a stool and looked around. The decor was French rustic and included the mounted heads of several bucks and three stuffed birds: two pheasants and an owl.

"I can't stay for dinner," Tysin said.

Mason turned toward the bar again and with his hand, he signaled the barkeep.

"Did you know that our friend suffers from claustrophobia?" Tysin asked, looking at Mason's reflection.

"He can't be!" Mason exclaimed.

"I have someone who I think might testify that he does," Tysin said in a low voice.

"Who?"

The barkeep came over to where Tysin and Mason were seated.

"I'll have another," Tysin said.

"And you sir, what will you have?" the barkeep asked Mason.

"Chivas on the rocks," Mason answered.

The barkeep moved away.

"A woman," Tysin answered, gathering a handful of peanuts from a wooden bowl. "The TV reporter Linda Johnson."

"And I thought I had news for you," Mason responded. "How the hell did you find that out?"

Tysin gave him an enigmatic smile, but said nothing.

The barkeep returned with their drinks.

Mason removed a twenty dollar bill from his wallet and put it on the bar. "Take them out of that," he said.

"Will do," the barkeep answered and picking up the twenty, he went to the cash register.

"That could be it," Mason said. "That and what I have. I have someone who's anxious to get ahead."

"From the crew?"

"Lieutenant Michael Lipner," Mason said.

Tysin nodded approvingly.

"How far will the lieutenant be willing to go?"

The waiter returned with the change and put it on the bar in front of Mason, smiled and then walked away.

"As far as we want him to go," Mason answered.

"Was he on the bridge the night of the accident?"

"No. He was at the COMCOMP below deck. The only other officer on the bridge with Boxer was Cowly."

"Did he notice anything unusual about Boxer immediately before the accident?" Tysin asked.

"I'm sure he did," Mason said, lifting his glass.

Tysin smiled, lifted his glass and touched Mason's with it. "I think we have something going," he said.

"It looks that way, doesn't it," Mason said.

Reaching for another handful of peanuts, Tysin asked, "Is there anything else?"

Mason started to shake his head and say *no*, but instead he said, "Remember that young sailor who was with Boxer and broke into the *Shark*'s computers?"

"Donald Butts," Tysin said. "He's got a presidential appointment to Annapolis. What about him?"

"Came up dead with a knife in his chest."

"Where?"

"Crayville."

"Where the hell is that?"

"The eastern part of Virginia. From the preliminary MO report he was killed in the water."

"Who found him?" Tysin asked.

"A call came into the local police chief. I spoke to him on the phone. He doesn't sound all that bright."

"Tough break for the kid," Tysin said.

"Tougher on the family," Mason responded.

"Have you notified Boxer that a member of his crew was murdered?" Tysin asked.

"Tomorrow. We just found out about it ourselves this afternoon."

"Will he have to ID the body?"

"Could be requested to make the ID," Mason said.

"Do it. It will help keep him off balance and the more he's off balance, the better off we are."

"Cowly is being buried tomorrow," Mason said.

Tysin nodded. "Then have Boxer make the ID tomorrow." He looked at his watch and said, "I'm really sorry I can't stay and have dinner with you."

"We'll make it another time," Mason responded.

Tysin started to reach for his wallet.

"I'm buying; you can do it next time," Mason told him.

"Thanks," Tysin said, stood up and turning, he walked away.

Mason half turned and watched him. The man even moved differently from the way he had just a few days before. Something had changed in his life; something was giving him a youthful bounce and that something, Mason was certain, had to be a woman.

He turned back to the bar and lifting his drink, he decided that it might be a good thing for him to know who the woman was. After all, even if it's just something to rub his nose in from time to time, it would be worth knowing. And if it should turn out to be more than just a fucking party, so much the better. Mason had no doubt that Tysin was a snake and he also had no doubt that the only way to handle a snake was to defang him. He reached for the peanuts, but the bowl was empty. "How about another drink and some peanuts down here," he called out.

"Yes, sir. Coming right up!" the barkeep answered.

Mason turned around, looked at the hat check girl and wondered if he had the chance of scoring with a woman that young.

"A Chivas on the rocks and a bowl of peanuts," the barkeep said, setting them down in front of Mason.

"Has the hat check girl worked here long?" Mason asked.

"A couple of weeks," the barkeep answered.

"Do you know if she has a boyfriend?"

The man shook his head.

"Suppose I wanted to meet her, do you think you could arrange it?" Mason asked.

The man smiled. "I could arrange it," he said.

"Then arrange it," Mason told him and he handed him a twenty dollar bill.

"When will you leave?" Tanya asked, holding on to Borodine's arm as they walked along the outside of Gorky Park.

"I wasn't given a specific date," Borodine answered, his breath steaming in the frigid air. "I imagine it will be as soon as the *Sea Dragon* is ready."

Tanya didn't answer.

Knowing what was on her mind, Borodine said, "Maybe we'll get lucky and I won't have to leave until after the baby is born."

"Can't you meet your ship somewhere?" she asked.

Borodine suppressed a smile. "It's not as easy as that," he said. "After she's repaired, she must be tested again."

Again Tanya was silent.

"I told you," he said gently, "that it wouldn't be an easy life."

She nodded. "Yes, you told me. But I didn't think I'd fall in love with you and —"

Borodine stopped, turned her toward him and kissed her. "And I've fallen in love with you. But I also have my duty to perform." He took hold of her arm and started to walk again. "This time when I leave Moscow, I want you to go to my parents and stay with them. They'll take good care of you."

"They'll spoil me," Tanya responded.

"No more than I would, if I were home," Borodine said with a laugh.

"You know, as much as I love being in Moscow, I really would rather be back home," she told him. "Here, everything is so dense. You can't go out in the street and not see other people. But at home — well, you don't have to see anyone, if you don't want to."

"You should have told me that before," Borodine said. "I would —"

"No... No... I understand that you must be here. But I do like our village. The village would be a better place to raise a child than a small apartment in a very large building."

Borodine rubbed his beard. "To tell the truth, I really haven't thought about raising the baby yet. I mean, it's not even here yet."

"Ah, but it is," Tanya answered, patting her extended stomach. "It's here and doing very well, thank you."

Borodine laughed and said, "Then we'll raise him in the village."

"Would you be very upset if —"

"A girl. No. Not, as long as she's like you."

Tanya squeezed his arm and said in a low voice, "Igor, I have something I want to ask you and I want you to promise that you won't become angry."

"How could I promise that?"

"Promise, please!"

"All right, I promise."

"Would you mind if I had the child baptized?" Tanya asked.

"Baptized!" Borodine exclaimed.

"I know you don't believe," Tanya said, "and neither do I."

"Then why —"

"My mother died believing," Tanya explained. "I want to do it for her memory. We don't ever have to tell the child. But I'd like to give it my mother's name and —"

"The KGB will find out," Borodine said. "The two of us are Party members. I'd certainly be asked to explain why my child was baptized."

"I didn't mean baptized in the Russian Church," Tanya answered.

"Then what church?"

"The Catholic," she said.

"Your mother was a Catholic?"

"She was Polish," Tanya answered. "My father was Russian. He met my mother just before the war with Germany."

"But where are you going to get a priest here?" Borodine asked.

"Not here. In Poland. We'll go to Poland. I have relatives there. Aunts, uncles, even cousins."

"You never told me that before," Borodine said.

She shrugged. "There really wasn't any reason to. Besides, we never really had the time to sit down and talk about ourselves."

Borodine nodded and realized that he knew very little about Tanya and she knew less about him. They had married because both of them wanted to marry and they were lucky enough to have fallen in love.

"You don't have to answer now," Tanya said. "Think about it and then tell me."

"I don't have to think about it," he said. "If it will make you happy, do it."

"Oh Igor, are you sure?"

"I'm sure," he said resolutely. "Now let's go home, I'm freezing."

"So am I."

"Why didn't you tell me?"

"I thought you wanted to walk," she said.

173

"What I want to do is go home and make love to you," Borodine said.

"Why didn't you tell me?" she asked.

"I thought you wanted to walk," he said.

The two of them began to laugh and quickened their pace.

The day the hearings began it started to snow some time around two in the morning. Boxer was awake. He stood at the window and watched the flakes instantly melt when they touched the window. Several years ago, when his ship the *Sting Ray* had been involved in an accident with Sanchez's yacht, he had undergone a similar hearing. In fact that was how he had met Sanchez. But that really had been an accident. The captain and the helmsman had been drunk. But what happened with the *Barracuda* was very different. Someone was trying to destroy her. Trying —

"Are you all right?" Francine asked, from the bed.

Boxer turned toward her. "I thought I'd watch the snow fall," he lied.

"Is it really snowing?" she asked, pulling herself up on her elbows and resting on them.

"Really is."

"The city is going to be a mess if it sticks," she commented and leaning over to the night table she looked at the green numbers of the digital clock. "It's only ten after two!" she exclaimed.

Boxer faced the window again.

"Come back to bed," Francine said. "It's not going to be an easy day for you."

"I can't put it together," Boxer said. "Only the Russians would benefit from the destruction of the *Barracuda*, but so far it doesn't seem as if they had a hand in it."

"You're assuming that," she said.

"It's not their style. To go back the next day and plant the evidence. If they had been involved, that motorboat would have actually smashed into the *Barracuda*. The people they use for that kind of work are professionals. They would have known what had to be done and wouldn't have risked going back to cover their mistake."

Francine pulled herself up into a sitting position and rested her back against the headboard. "Let's assume you're right," she said, "then you would have to assume that some other country or group could have been responsible."

"That is exactly what I do think."

"Any ideas what country or group?"

"The Libyans certainly would be high on my list. One of their generals swore to kill me."

"Say that again," Francine said.

Boxer repeated what he had just said.

"That might be where the answer is," Francine told him.

He faced her again.

"I know, considering what happened, it's a way out idea," she said. "But just suppose that it is true. Just suppose," she continued, bringing her knees up and hugging them, "that you and only you were the target?"

"I'd say that who ever tried —"

"Knew he'd missed with the first missile —"

"The first missile hit amidship," Boxer said.

"That's right. He knew that and he probably guessed you'd be on the outside bridge. That was what he really wanted to hit with the first missile and that was why he had to fire a second."

"He certainly killed a lot of men to get at me," Boxer said in a low, sad voice.

"What do you think of the idea?"

"A possibility," Boxer said.

"Is it plausible?"

"Yes. If someone really wanted to waste me, I guess that's one way of doing it. But it would be a lot easier to do it on the street."

"Easier, perhaps. But certainly making it seem that you were killed accidentally would provide perfect cover for the murderer."

"I can't argue with that," Boxer said.

"It's something to bring up at the hearing."

Boxer was silent.

"Well isn't it?" Francine asked.

"Not if someone is still trying to kill me," Boxer said. "It would put him on guard. Whatever I say will be reported." He went from the window to the bed and sat down on it.

"Do you think it could have been the Libyans?" Francine asked.

Boxer eased himself down into a supine position. "They might have tried," he said.

Francine settled down next to him. "They'll try again, won't they?" she asked.

"One way or another," Boxer answered.

"Aren't you frightened?"

"Yes, but there's nothing I can do about it."

"You could ask for protection?"

"From whom?"

"The Navy? The Company? They'd certainly have to do something if you told Mason, or Tysin."

"I guess they would," he said.

"Then tell them, Jack. Your life is at stake."

"Maybe it is and maybe it's not, at least not now. Not when I'm in the public eye, so to speak."

"But you said whoever tried to kill you will try again."

"Not now."

"How can you be sure of that?"

"They've tried to make it look like an accident," Boxer said. "They want to cover their tracks."

"But as soon as you tell the Board about the missiles, they'll know —"

"They'll know I know it wasn't an accident. But I'll also have to tell the Board in sequence that prior to being hit by the missiles, I spotted a Russian fishing trawler and radioed her position to the base operations."

"I don't see what that will do."

"It will make everyone think somehow the missiles came from trawler," Boxer said.

"What about the wreckage the Navy divers found?"

"What about it?" Boxer asked.

"No games, please," Francine said. "Just tell me how you intend to explain that?"

"I don't," Boxer said. "When that is brought up as evidence, I will tell the Board that I can't explain the presence of the wreckage and I will suggest that the *Barracuda* be examined for crash marks, or any other indications that she might have been struck by another craft."

"Are you saying —"

"There aren't any marks for them to find," Boxer said. "I went over her with my EO after I ID'd DB's body."

"I almost forgot you had to do that," she said sympathetically.

"I'd rather not talk about it."

She took hold of his hand and squeezed it tightly.

"The members of the Board will either accept my statement, or examine the *Barracuda* themselves. Either way they're going to have to question whether the wreckage was placed there by someone and if it was, why was it?"

"If they go that far, they'll have to believe your statement about the missiles."

"Yes," Boxer said. "It would be the only alternative they have."

"But everything will still point to the Russians?"

"Yes, for now," Boxer said.

"And that will be the end of the hearing?" Francine asked.

"That should be the end of it," Boxer said. "I can't think of anything else that might come up."

"You worked this out pretty neatly. I mean, considering you're not a member of the legal profession, I'd have to say you've presented an excellent defense for yourself."

"I think so too," Boxer said.

"No need to be smug about it."

"Not smug," Boxer answered, "just pleased that I have something to get myself off the hook. More than twenty men died as a result of those missiles and I want to find out who ordered them launched."

"And when you do find out, what could you do about it?"

"There's no sense talking about that now," Boxer said. "I may never find out. But you can be sure that if I do," he added, his voice going hard, "you can be sure that I'll get them."

"Kill them?" she questioned in a whisper.

Boxer didn't answer.

It was eight-thirty in the morning. The President was already at his desk in the Oval Office. Both Mason and Tysin were seated directly in front of him. "Thank you for coming on such short notice," he said. "But I wanted you to know my feelings about the hearings that will begin later this morning."

Mason glanced at Tysin.

"I know they must be held, considering the nature of the accident," the President said. "But I'd like you to know that I would prefer them to go smoothly."

"I'm afraid I don't understand what you mean by *go smoothly*?" Tysin said.

"Boxer is too valuable a man to let something like this —"

"But if negligence could be proved, then certainly he must be punished," Mason said.

"I'll make my position clearer," the President said, "I don't want Boxer touched. I will personally intercede on his behalf should the hearings fail to go smoothly. Have I made myself clear?"

"You certainly have," Mason answered.

"Mister President, may I ask you why you've taken this position?" Tysin asked.

"I have my reasons and I assure you they are in the best interests of the country."

"Mister President, may I take the liberty of reminding you that Admiral Boxer embarrassed you in front of the —"

The President held up his hand. "Gentlemen, I know you have busy schedules. I have one too. You know my feelings in the matter and you have my word that I will intervene if the hearings make any recommendations that will in any way endanger Admiral Boxer's career."

Tysin and Mason rose in unison.

The President smiled at them and said, "Have a pleasant day."

"The very same to you," Tysin answered, unable to keep the growl out of his voice.

Mason nodded and said, "Good morning."

Within moments they were in the hallway and on their way to their limos. Neither one spoke until they were outside of the White House. There was a light coating of snow on the sidewalk and on the bare limbs of the trees.

Tysin stopped before he reached his limo and said, "Someone got to him."

"Who?"

"I sure as hell am going to find out," Tysin answered.

"What are we going to do?"

"Exactly what we planned to do," Tysin said. "Maybe we can make it go so rough for Boxer that the President will have to back down. I don't want Boxer to get away. I want to finish him off."

Mason nodded.


The room where the hearing was held was too small for the number of spectators, most of whom were members of the press. The Navy forbade TV coverage inside the room but the network hotshots were gathered outside with their cameramen and sound technicians.

The members of the board consisted of Admirals John Dickens, Peter Hawthorne, Arthur Twain and Robert Melville. None of them had ever had submarine commands. Admiral Dickens was the presiding officer and Admiral Melville was in command of the Coast Guard district that included the Chesapeake Bay area. They sat at a long table in the front of the room. In the center of the table was a metal tray on which there was a pitcher of water surrounded by as many glasses as there were members of the board and an extra one for the witness, should he become thirsty.

In front of each officer was a pad of yellow paper and four freshly sharpened pencils. On their left was the flag, to their right was the Navy standard. Directly behind them, on the wall, a framed eleven by fourteen photograph of the President.

Boxer and his crew occupied the first four rows of seats facing the members of the board and separated from them by a space of twenty feet in which there was a metal folding chair where the individual being questioned would sit.

Because the helmsman, Mahony, was the only other survivor of the bridge detail beside Boxer, he was the first witness called.

After he was sworn in and gave his name, rank and duty, he was asked by Admiral Dickens to tell the board where he was at the time of the crash.

"At the helm," Mahony answered.

"How far were you from Admiral Boxer?" Dickens asked.

"No more than four feet."

"To the port or starboard side?"

"Directly aft of him, sir," Mahony answered.

"And at the time of the crash Admiral Boxer had the CONN?"

"Yes, sir."

"In your own words will you tell the members of the board exactly what took place?"

"There was this throbbing sound coming from somewhere off our port side and —"

"Excuse me, Petty Officer Mahony," Admiral Hawthorne said, "but are you sure that the sound was off your port side?"

"Yes, sir."

"Continue," Admiral Dickens said.

"Well sir, the skipper, I mean Admiral Boxer checked with the RO to see if there was anything on the scope."

"Was there?"

"No. Whatever was out there was probably lying too low in the water for us to pick up. The sound kept getting louder and louder."

"Did Admiral Boxer give you any orders to change course?"

"No. Not until he saw it."

"Do you remember what his order was?"

"Hard right. Hard right."

"Did he say anything else?"

"He said, 'It's changing course. It's coming after us!'"

"Did he do anything else?"

"He went to flank speed," Mahony answered.

"How long a period of time would you guess passed before Admiral Boxer saw the oncoming craft and ordered you to change course?"

"A few seconds at most."

"And how long did it take for the ship to respond to the helm?" Admiral Melville asked.

"No more than thirty seconds," Mahony answered. "She's very responsive."

"What happened after the crash?" Admiral Dickens asked.

"The skipper and Mister Cowly, God rest his soul, were busy trying to find out how much damage had been done and if there were any casualties."

"Did Admiral Boxer give you any additional orders?" Admiral Hawthorne questioned.

"Not then. Not until after the second explosion."

"Where was that explosion?"

"Somewhere below us on the sail."

"Was that the explosion that killed Mister Cowly?"

"Yes," Mahony answered in a low voice. "It killed him and the others on the bridge."

"What was Admiral Boxer's second order?" Admiral Melville asked.

"To turn inshore."

"To beach the *Barracuda*?"

"Yes, sir."

"Is there anything else you'd like to tell the board?" Admiral Dickens asked.

"No, sir. I mean —"

"If you think it has any bearing on what happened, you must tell us," Admiral Dickens said.

"There was another sound beside the throbbing sound of a high-speed motorboat," Mahony said. "There was a high-pitched scream twice."

Boxer suppressed a smile. He would have been willing to bet that Mahony had heard it too.

"I don't understand," Admiral Melville said. "Would you explain where those high-pitched screams came from."

"I don't know where they came from, sir," Mahony said. "They were just there."

"Before or after the crash?"

"Before the explosions, sir."

Melville looked questioningly at the other members of the board and then asked Mahony, "If you were to describe the sound in some other way other than the way you have already described it, what would you say about it?"

Mahony took several moments before he said, "It sounded like the scream of a missile."

"Are you sure that's the way you'd describe it?"

"Yes, sir," Mahony answered.

"The witness may stand down," Dickens said. "But he must hold himself ready to appear before the board at any time during the time it sits."

"Yes, sir," Mahony answered.

Boxer was called next and after he was sworn in Admiral Dickens began the questioning by asking him to explain to the court the situation before the crash.

"The *Barracuda* surfaced just before we entered Chesapeake Bay," Boxer said. "There was a heavy fog. Visibility was limited to maybe fifty yards at the most and at times less than that. Our navigational radar was in operation as well as our surface acquisition radar."

"Did you pick up any targets within the operating range of your radar?"

"Target acquisition picked up a Russian trawler."

"Are you sure it was Russian?"

"It was computer ID'd," Boxer answered.

"Were there any other targets?"

"Negative."

"When you ID'd the Russian trawler, what did you do?"

"I had my Radio Officer contact Base OP and give its OD the trawler's coordinates."

"Why did you do that?"

"To have it frightened off by our planes," Boxer answered. "The Russians often use their fishing vessels to track the movements of our incoming and outgoing submarines and other craft."

"Then is the board to understand you've had similar experiences with Russian fishing trawlers at other times?"

"Yes."

"Now will you tell the board what the situation was immediately before the crash?"

"There was suddenly a throbbing sound off our port side," Boxer said. "The sound became louder and suddenly there was a high-speed motorboat heading straight for us amidships."

"How far away would you say it was from the *Barracuda* before you saw it?" Admiral Hawthorne asked.

"A hundred yards at the very most," Boxer said.

"But you yourself just said the visibility was down to fifty yards and at times less than that."

"The visibility in fog changes moment by moment," Boxer answered. "I would say that when I first saw the motorboat it was at least a hundred yards away."

"Given that it was a hundred yards away, would you say that at the speed it was traveling that the *Barracuda* could have avoided a collision by going hard to the starboard?"

"In my judgment at flank speed, yes."

"Your judgment, Admiral, apparently was none too good considering the fact that the *Barracuda* did not evade the oncoming motorboat."

"With all due respect," Boxer answered calmly, "the *Barracuda* did evade the motorboat."

"Then how do you explain the disaster that took the lives of twenty of your crew?" Admiral Dickens snapped.

Boxer ignored the question and said, "Yesterday I and my EO made a thorough examination of the *Barracuda*'s exterior. Nowhere on her is there any evidence of her having been involved in a crash with any type of craft, especially a high-speed motorboat."

"Admiral, we have absolute proof that the *Barracuda* was struck by a high-speed motorboat. Navy divers have recovered the motorboat's wreckage."

"The divers certainly did recover the wreckage of a high-speed motorboat, but that boat and the *Barracuda* never made contact. The board only has to ask the ship's EO if he found any crash marks anywhere on the *Barracuda*, or make the examination themselves."

The members of the board whispered among themselves and Admiral Dickens said, "The board is willing to provisionally accept your statement, but only if you explain to its satisfaction how the wreckage was found in the exact place where the crash took place."

"It was put there," Boxer answered.

"By whom?" Admiral Hawthorne asked.

"By the same person or persons who fired the missiles at the *Barracuda*," Boxer said. His answer caused an immediate stir in the courtroom.

Admiral Dickens picked up a gavel, rapped it twice and said, "I will have this room cleared of all spectators if I do not have it quiet." Then to Boxer, he said, "I hope you are able to prove the statement you just made, Admiral."

Boxer nodded. "As Petty Officer Mahony has already told the board, there were two high-pitched screams and each of them preceded an explosion."

"By what length of time?" Admiral Melville asked.

"Between the explosions?"

"Between the time you heard the high-pitched sound and the explosion?"

"Twenty seconds at the most," Boxer answered.

"And between explosions?"

"Two minutes, perhaps. At the very most three minutes," Boxer answered.

"Is it your contention," Admiral Hawthorne asked, "that the *Barracuda* was struck by two missiles and not by a high-speed motorboat?"

"Yes, sir, that's exactly my contention."

"And that the missiles were fired from the motorboat you saw?"

"Yes, sir."

"And is it also your contention that the motorboat came from the Russian trawler you had ID'd earlier?"

"No sir, that is a conclusion that you arrived at," Boxer answered.

"And what conclusion did you arrive at with regard to where the motorboat came from?" Admiral Dickens asked.

"I did not arrive at any conclusion about the origin of the motorboat," Boxer said.

"But you did go to great pains to indicate that the *Barracuda* was not struck by a motorboat and therefore the wreckage that was recovered by navy divers was not the wreckage of the motorboat that attacked the *Barracuda*, but was planted there by certain individuals for the purpose of influencing the board."

"I wanted to show the members of the board that the *Barracuda* had not been involved in an accident and the disaster that had occurred had not been due to my, or any other officer's negligence."

"The board understands that," Admiral Dickens said. "And I must admit you have presented very strong evidence to back your assertion that neither you, nor any other officer aboard the *Barracuda* was responsible for what had happened. But I for one would like you to tell the board who you think was responsible for launching the missiles?"

"I am not able to do that," Boxer answered.

"Admiral," Dickens said, "I think you can tell us, but for special reasons of your own, you will not say openly that those missiles were fired from a high-speed Russian motorboat."

"That is conjecture," Boxer answered.

"But it isn't conjecture, Admiral, in fact it is a matter of public information that you and Admiral Igor Borodine are very good friends."

"I should hope we are good friends," Boxer answered. "We have certainly demonstrated that friendship many, many times over the past few years. But may I say something more on the subject of my friendship with Comrade Admiral Igor Borodine?"

"I have no objections to hearing more on the subject," Admiral Dickens said.

"There isn't a man aboard the *Barracuda* who does not owe his life to Comrade Admiral Igor Borodine and his crew and in like manner there is not a man aboard the *Sea Dragon* who does not owe his life to the efforts of the men aboard the *Barracuda*." He turned to his crew and asked, "Have I told the board the truth?"

"You told it like it is, Skipper," one of the men answered.

The others agreed.

Boxer faced the board again. "I leave you and others to draw whatever conclusion you can about the origin of the motorboat. I cannot say where it came from. I can only tell the board with absolute certainty that the *Barracuda* was struck by two low flying surface-to-surface missiles and not by any high-speed motorboat."

Admiral Dickens asked the other members if they had any more questions for Admiral Boxer.

"I have one," Admiral Hawthorne said.

Admiral Dickens nodded.

Admiral Hawthorne picked up several sheets of paper. "I have here two sworn statements from two different individuals, one of whom is an officer under your command aboard the *Barracuda*, that you suffer from a severe case of claustrophobia."

An excited murmur suddenly filled the room.

Admired Dickens rapped the gavel three times. "There must be silence in the room," he admonished, or I will clear it of all spectators."

Boxer's heart began to race. He began to sweat.

"Did you ever report your condition to your superior?" Hawthorne asked.

"Admiral Stark was aware of it," Boxer answered.

"Did you report it to the present CNO?" Hawthorne pressed.

"In my considered opinion," Boxer heard himself say, "the difficulty was under control."

"How? By medication? By any sort of professional treatment?"

"No," Boxer answered. "I brought it under control —"

"Admiral, according to the two statements I hold in my hand, you did not bring it under control and that when you were suffering from a claustrophobic attack, you were less than rational. According to the sworn statement made by one of your officers, you had an attack on the night of the disaster."

"I did not," Boxer answered quickly.

"This officer claims that you were the first one on the bridge because you could not stand being confined in the narrow space of the *Barracuda*."

"I was the first man on the bridge because I was the one who happened to open the hatch," Boxer answered.

"Is that usual?"

"Aboard the *Barracuda* we do not bother with the usual," Boxer answered. "If something has to be done and I can do it, I will do it."

"Ah, then rank has no privileges, is that right?"

"Only the privilege of command, nothing more," Boxer answered.

"So you, knowing full well that you suffered from a difficulty that in an emergency might render you totally useless, accepted the privilege of command, even though it might, and for all we know did, imperil your crew and boat?"

Boxer was suddenly numb. He had told no one aboard the *Barracuda* about his claustrophobic attacks and had done everything possible to —

"Admiral, you haven't answered the question, or perhaps your silence should be taken as a *shameful yes*?"

"I ask the board's permission," Boxer said, "to question the individuals whose statements Admiral Hawthorne has used to question my ability to command during specific situations."

Again the members of the board conferred and Admiral Dickens said, "the board wants to remind Admiral Boxer that it is not sitting in judgment of his actions and that its only action is to listen to, and consider, the facts presented to it and from this consideration recommend a course of action to the Navy."

"The facts," Boxer responded, "are exactly what I hope to give the board by questioning the two individuals whose statements have questioned my ability to command."

"The board calls Ms. Linda Johnson to the witness chair," Admiral Dickens said.

Boxer stood up and turned around. He was not surprised to hear her name.

She stepped out into the aisle and walked forward. She wore a light gray dress that clung to her body.

Every head was turned toward her.

Boxer moved away from the chair and waited until she was seated.

Admiral Dickens said, "The board wants to thank you, Ms. Johnson, for your cooperation in this matter and wishes to remind you that though this is not a court of law, the same rules regarding perjury do apply."

She nodded and looked defiantly at Boxer.

"You may question Ms. Johnson, Admiral Boxer," Admiral Dickens said.

Boxer nodded. He looked at Linda for a moment and he asked, "Would you recall for the board how we happened to meet?"

"Before or after your claustrophobic attack?" she responded.

"On the day that it happened," Boxer said.

"I was waiting for you —"

"Wouldn't it be more accurate to say that you waylaid me while I was on my way out of my hotel?"

"I was waiting —"

"Ms. Johnson, did we have an appointment?"

"I don't remember," she said.

"I do. We did not have an appointment. But you wanted to do an exclusive interview about me. Where did we go from the lobby of my hotel?"

"We walked."

"We did indeed walk to your apartment. Do you recall why? I will quote then your exact words. 'I'm getting tired of walking, and I feel kind of horny.'"

An explosion of comments came from the men of the *Barracuda*.

Dickens used his gavel again to quiet the room.

Her face was flushed.

"We're now in your apartment," Boxer said, "will you tell the board what happened there?"

"You started acting weird," she said.

"Exactly what do you mean by weird?"

"Strange?"

"Did we screw, Ms. Johnson?"

"I don't remember," she said.

"Ms. Johnson, you're a very beautiful woman and I assure that if we had screwed, I would have remembered it."

The room exploded with laughter.

Dickens rapped three times with his gavel and looking at Boxer, he said, "Please make your point, Admiral."

"My point is, sir, that Ms. Johnson is here out of anger, or for reasons I can't even begin to guess at. We did go to her apartment for the express purpose of having sex, but it was there that I had my first claustrophobic attack and I could not have intercourse with her." Then looking at Linda, he asked, "Isn't that so, Ms. Johnson?"

"You were weird," she said.

"Did we have sex?"

She hesitated. "We started —"

Boxer leaned close to her. "Did we ever get into bed? Were either of us naked?"

"No," she said in a low voice.

"Louder," he said.

"No," she shouted. "There, are you satisfied now?"

Boxer took a deep breath and slowly exhaled. "Not yet, Ms. Johnson. I'd like you to tell the board who your half-sister was."

"I don't see what that has to do with anything," she answered.

"If you don't, I will. But it would be better if you did," Boxer said.

"My half-sister was Tracy Kimble," she said.

"And what was my relationship to Tracy?" Boxer asked.

"You were lovers," Linda said.

Boxer looked at the board. "Tracy was murdered several years ago," he explained; then he added, "The board can now draw its own conclusions as to the reason why Ms. Johnson came forward with the information that I was claustrophobic. Somewhere I remember reading the words, 'Hell hath no fury like a woman scorned.' I don't have any more questions for Ms. Johnson."

"Ms. Johnson," Admiral Dickens said, "thank you for agreeing to be a witness and thank you for giving the board your sworn statement. You may stand down."

She left the chair and without looking at Boxer, Linda walked quickly down the aisle and out of the room.

Admiral Dickens waited until the door closed after her, before he said, "Admiral, you may have proved to the board that Ms. Johnson's actions were considerably less than those of a responsible person, but you did nothing to obviate the fact that you do suffer from claustrophobia and that you failed to report it to the proper authorities."

Boxer nodded. "I only want to indicate to the court that Ms. Johnson's motives for her actions were questionable. Now, if I may question the other individual whose statement Admiral Hawthorne has?"

"Will Lieutenant Michael Lipner come forward," Admired Dickens said.

Boxer glanced questioningly at Dickens and then looked at Lipner. He had recently given the man an excellent fitness rating and recommended that he be promoted to the rank of lieutenant commander. At one time, he remembered Cowly having said something about Lipner's excessive ambition.

After Lipner was sworn in and been reminded by Admiral Dickens that the board could only hear statements, and based on those statements make specific recommendations, Boxer stepped close to Lipner and said, "I will not ask you to identify yourself, or state your rank. But I will ask you to tell the board at what time and in what circumstance did you see me in a condition where I could not function?"

"During our last mission, when we were under attack from Russian surface craft," Lipner said.

Boxer flushed.

"You were sweating profusely and were very pale," Lipner said. "And I do believe you were trembling."

For several moments, Boxer looked hard at him and then he asked, "Where is your battle station with regard to the COMCOMP?"

"Behind the COMCOMP," Lipner answered. "But I saw you when you turned to speak to Mister Cowly."

"You didn't happen to hear what I said to Mister Cowly, did you?"

"No."

"How far away would you say your station is from the COMCOMP?"

"Eight feet at the most."

"And how far away would you say Mister Cowly's station was?"

"About the same distance," Lipner answered.

"Did Mister Cowly hear what I said?" Boxer asked.

"I think so," Lipner said, touching his small moustache. He was a short, wiry man with thinning brown hair and bright brown eyes that nervously darted from Boxer to the board and back to Boxer again.

"You're not sure then?"

Lipner remained silent.

"Did Mister Cowly respond to what I said?"

"He activated —"

"Tell the board what Mister Cowly did," Boxer said in a flat hard voice.

"He pressed the Killer Dart Fire Control Button," Lipner answered.

"In response to what I said?"

"Yes."

"But you didn't hear me give that order?"

"No."

"Would Mister Cowly have taken it upon himself to press the Killer Dart Fire Control Button?"

"No. You had to shift control from the COMCOMP to his computer station."

Boxer looked at the board. "To make that shift, gentlemen, required that I change several control settings and if I was unfit to command, as Mister Lipner claims, I could not have either changed those settings, or issued an order to Mister Cowly."

"There were other times when you —" Lipner began.

Boxer glared him into silence; then he said, "I have a few more questions, Mister Lipner, before you step down. You obviously stated that because of my condition, I was the first one out on the bridge the night we surfaced before we entered the Chesapeake Bay?"

"That was the way it seemed to me," Lipner said sullenly.

"Did I look ill before we surfaced?"

"You looked anxious," Lipner answered.

Boxer nodded. "What would you say if I said that you looked anxious too and so did every man aboard the *Barracuda* look anxious, as you put it. That anxious look comes from realizing that very soon we'll be home again and in another world, a world not bounded by the steel hull of the *Barracuda* and the ocean that lies beyond it."

"You ran for the hatchway," Lipner said.

"Lieutenant, there are other men here who would disagree with you."

"I can't comment on that," Lipner said.

"Suppose you're right. Suppose I did run for the hatchway. Would that indicate that I was too ill to perform my duty?"

"It would if you were having a claustrophobic attack," Lipner answered.

"Yes, you're probably right," Boxer said. "But I wasn't having another attack. Petty Officer Mahony came up on the bridge directly behind me and I am sure if the question was put to him, as to whether or not I was able to command, his answer would be that I was not only able to command, but I did command."

"Mister Lipner," Admiral Dickens said, "your statements are more your opinion than hard fact."

"If it please the board, I have one more question I want to ask the witness."

"Go ahead," Admiral Dickens said.

"Lieutenant Lipner, is it unusual for the first man on the way to the topside bridge to run, or does he go up the ladder at a leisurely pace?"

Lipner hesitated.

"Let me answer the question for you," Boxer said. "On all occasions, when the boat is underway, officers and men alike go topside as quickly as possible. Isn't that so Lieutenant?"

"Yes," Lipner answered.

"Would you please tell the board why this is SOP," Boxer said.

"Command must be transferred as quickly as possible from the inside bridge to the topside bridge," Lipner responded.

Boxer looked at the members of the board. "I don't have any more questions," Boxer told them.

"Lieutenant Lipner, you may stand down," Admiral Dickens said.

Lipner stood up and for a moment he looked as if he would say something to Boxer, but then he turned around and walked back to where he had been seated. The men on either side of him stood up and moved away.

Boxer sat down in the witness chair again.

"You may stand down, Admiral Boxer," Dickens said. "But you must remain available for the remainder of this hearing."

Boxer nodded, stood up and walked to a chair on the aisle. Those men sitting close by reached over and touched him and one whispered, "Good going, Skipper."

Shortly before twelve-thirty Admiral Dickens called a recess for lunch and said, "This hearing will reconvene at fourteen hundred hours."


In the hall, outside the room where the hearing was held, Boxer was mobbed by TV reporters. All of them wanted a statement from him.

"I have nothing to say," he told them. "Everything I had to say I said during the hearing."

"Do you think the two missiles came from —" one of the reporters started to ask.

"I'm not prepared to say where they came from," Boxer said.

"What are your feelings with regard to Linda Johnson?" another TV network person asked.

"If you were in my place," Boxer countered, "what would your feelings be?"

"Will you allow Lieutenant Lipner to serve under you again?" a third reporter asked.

"That is not my decision to make," Boxer answered. "Personnel makes all the assignments."

"Surely you could request his transfer?"

"I feel certain that Mister Lipner will request his own transfer," Boxer answered.

"And will you grant it?"

"I cannot answer that question now," Boxer responded.

"How do you think the Navy will respond to your claustrophobia?" the same reporter asked.

"I cannot say," Boxer replied and quickly added, "Now if you will excuse me, I have a lunch date with members of my crew." And without waiting for a response, Boxer launched himself forward and was quickly surrounded by a half dozen officers from the *Barracuda*, who escorted him out of the building.

The hearings started promptly at fourteen hundred and moved very swiftly, as every member of the crew was called to give a statement about what had happened to the *Barracuda*. By seventeen thirty it was over and Admiral Dickens said, "The hearing is over and the members of the board will study the facts and make its recommendations to the proper authorities. The board thanks the crew of the *Barracuda* and its commanding officer for being cooperative."

Boxer stood up and turned around. Francine and Stark were sitting in the last row on the aisle. He smiled at them.

"Well, Skipper," his EO said, "I think we gave them one hell of a good fight."

"I think so too," Boxer answered.

Several of the other men said the same thing to him and then Mahony approached him and said, "Skipper, I almost didn't tell them about those high-pitched sounds. I thought I was goin' kind of nuts just thinkin' about them."

"I know what you mean," Boxer answered.

Mahony smiled. "But I'm sure as hell glad I did tell them."

"I'm sure as hell glad too," Boxer answered and he started to walk toward Francine and Stark. When he reached them, he said, "I thought I told the two of you not to come."

"Wouldn't listen," Stark answered in his gravelly voice. "Said something about not having to take orders."

"What about you?"

"I don't have to take orders either," Stark answered.

"Now can I say something?" Francine asked.

"Nothing," Boxer said, gathering her in his arms and kissing her on the lips. "Thanks for not paying any attention to what I told you."

"There you see!" Francine exclaimed, "I knew he really wanted us here." And she stuck out her tongue.

"That's unbecoming for a lady," Stark said.

Boxer laughed and shook Stark's hand. "Looks kind of cute," he said and then asked, "Where do the two of you want to go. I could use a drink and I'm hungry."

"Let's get out of here first," Francine said, possessively taking hold of Boxer by his arm. "The hallway is packed with TV and newspaper types."

Boxer nodded and said, "They might ask you some very embarrassing questions."

"About your relationship with Ms. Johnson?"

"How did you know —"

"Some of the exchange between the two of you is already on the boob tube and on radio," Francine explained. Then with a chuckle she added, "Neither one of us was a virgin when we met, were we?"

"Neither one," he answered.

"If you were, I certainly would have thought something was very wrong with you, especially since you had been married and had a son."

"And if you —"

"Will you stop all this virgin talk," Stark said, "and let's go for a drink and something to eat. I'm thirsty and hungry…

# CHAPTER 9

Tysin was in a fury. He paced back and forth across the length of his office, stopping now and then to glare at Mason. "I don't fucking believe it," he said. "I don't fucking believe that Boxer was able to do what he did at the hearing. But I blame myself. I really blame myself."

Mason stood up. He didn't like the idea that Tysin was taking him over the coals. Tysin was not his superior. The President, in his capacity as Commander in Chief was his superior and —

"There's more at stake in this than you know," Tysin blurted out.

Mason answered, "There certainly is with the Russians holding the smoking gun. Those missiles had to come from—"

"Boxer should have never —" he stopped himself.

Mason's brow furrowed. "Boxer should have never what?" he asked.

"It doesn't matter know," Tysin said. "Now we've got to figure out another way to get Boxer."

"Count me out," Mason said. "He's the President's fair-haired boy. You were there. He doesn't want anything to happen to him."

"And there must be a reason for that too," Tysin said, retreating behind his desk. "Will you sit down? I don't like speaking to someone who's standing while I'm seated."

Mason went to the chair and standing behind it, he rested his hands on the top of its black leather back. "I'm beginning to get a very uneasy feeling about all of this," he said.

"Uneasy about what?" Tysin asked, looking up at him.

"Your attitude toward various things."

"I don't see that we have a different attitude toward Boxer," Tysin answered. "You want to get rid of him just as much as I do."

Mason nodded. "Maybe even more. But I know when to back off. We underestimated him. He acted as if he was a trained lawyer. The board cannot ignore the facts. He proved that the *Barracuda* was not involved in a crash but was attacked."

"Then they must go for the claustrophobia," Tysin said viciously. "They must beat him over the head with it. Tell them… They're your boys. You told me you hand-picked them."

"The best you can hope for is a recommendation that Boxer be officially reprimanded."

"You have to be joking?"

Mason shook his head.

"For Christ sakes, will you sit down," Tysin exploded.

"No, I prefer to stand," Mason answered.

"An official reprimand, eh… And how do you think that will get rid of Boxer?"

"They might not even recommend that."

Tysin raised his eyebrows.

"There was no evidence given that his claustrophobia ever interfered with his ability to command."

"He did fail to notify you about his condition, didn't he?"

"I will put an official letter of reprimand in his personnel file and will note it on his next fitness report."

"That of course will have about as much effect as a fart in a windstorm," Tysin answered.

"The members of the board are well aware of public opinion," Mason said. "He's their hero."

"I'm beginning to get the idea that he might also be the board's hero," Tysin said in disgust.

"I certainly think they have a grudging admiration for him," Mason answered. "I know I do."

Tysin stared at him. "He thinks you're shit," he said in a tight voice.

Mason flushed.

"All right," Tysin said, "I might as well get used to the idea that we lost this one." He leaned forward and put his elbows on the desk. "But that doesn't mean we lost."

"Count me out," Mason said. "I'm going to have my hands full making sure that the Russians don't fire any more missiles in our backyard."

"You're making a big mistake," Tysin responded.

"No, I think you are. You've got Boxer on the brain. There's a hell of a lot more than Boxer to worry about," Mason said. He turned around and headed for the door. Before he reached it, he stopped and faced Tysin. "Just remember, like it or not, the President is your superior as well as mine and he has already told you that Boxer is off limits."

"I want it in writing," Tysin snarled.

Mason shrugged, turned toward the door again and in a few moments was out of the room. Tysin worried him and though he had thought about having him followed by NI, he hadn't given the necessary authorization. But now he made up his mind to do it as soon as he returned to the office. He was sure that Tysin was having an affair and for a man of Tysin's rigid morality, that must be monumentally unsettling.

Polyakov ordered his driver to stop the car. They were in a section of Moscow where the dregs of the Soviet economic system lived. Men and women, who lacked the skills or the intelligence to acquire them, spent their entire lives as either wards of the State, or performing the most menial of tasks.

Polyakov switched on the overhead light and looked at the piece of paper in his hand. The name of the street matched the name on the piece of paper. He turned off the overhead light, pocketed the piece of paper and said to his driver, "Move the car two streets up."

"Aye, aye, Comrade Admiral," his driver answered.

Polyakov left the car, walked to a narrow alleyway, hesitated and then entered it. Almost at the very end a small electric bulb glowed white over a doorway with three steps leading to it. The alleyway stank of garbage and urine. The walls on either side were brick and belonged to buildings that were probably built before the revolution, or immediately after it.

He mounted the three steps and opening the door, he stepped into a narrow, dimly lit hallway. But at the end of it not only was the light very bright but the sound that came from it was very loud and unmistakably American, something he'd learned from his last visit to Paris, called Rock.

Polyakov entered a room where dozens of young couples were gyrating to the beat of the music. There was so much smoke in the air that space just below the ceiling had a blue tinge. All of the people in the room were young and dressed in bright clothing.

He stood motionless and searched the tables along the wall, where he expected to see the man he had come to meet. But all of the tables were occupied. He wasn't sure whether or not he should enter, find a table and wait, or retreat toward the door and —

Suddenly he was aware that someone was behind him. He started to turn.

"Go in," the voice said. "Sit down at the third table from the wall. It's empty and there's a bottle of vodka on it and two glasses. Don't turn around."

Polyakov did as he was told.

Several of the women smiled at him.

He smiled back.

One of them came up to him, extended her hands and asked, "Do you want to dance?"

Taken aback, Polyakov couldn't find words, or his voice to answer.

"Come," she said, "come and enjoy yourself." She leaned close to him. "It's what you came for isn't it?" she asked.

Polyakov was afraid not to dance, lest he call attention to himself. He got to his feet and let himself be led to the center of the dance floor. "I'm afraid I won't be very good at this," he said.

"Just do what I do," the young woman answered, already gyrating.

Polyakov imitated her movements.

"Good," she said with a big smile and came close to him. "Your friend will be at the table by the time you return," she said.

Polyakov glanced at the table. No one was there yet.

"Enjoy the dance," she said, rubbing her breasts against his chest. "That can't be all bad," she teased.

"On the contrary," Polyakov answered with a smile, "it's very good, so good I'd like to have more."

"Greedy," she answered and turned around. When she faced him again, she said, "your friend is there. As soon as the music stops, we'll go our separate ways."

"Perhaps later —"

She shook her head, whirled around again and just as she faced him, the music stopped. "Go," she said, turned and walked away.

Polyakov made his way to the table and sat down opposite Valentine Makusky, the Deputy Director of the KGB's Second Directorate.

"Did you enjoy your dance?" Makusky asked. "I arranged it especially for you," he said with a smile. Makusky was a rosy-cheeked, avuncular looking man, with gray hair, horn-rimmed glasses that almost sat on the tip of his nose and enough of a stomach to indicate that he enjoyed eating and drinking.

"I enjoyed it very much," Polyakov answered.

"I could see that you did," Makusky said. "She's one of the best we have." He smiled. "This place is ours, too," he explained, as he poured vodka for himself. "This way we can keep track of those among the young people who might prove difficult in the future, or even now. We have a dossier on everyone who comes here."

Polyakov nodded approvingly.

"Now down to business," Makusky said.

Polyakov poured a vodka for himself. "Some friends of mine indicated that we have a mutual interest, or to put it more accurately we are interested in destroying a particular enemy of the State."

Makusky nodded. "I have many such interests," he said.

"This one is Comrade Admiral Igor Borodine," Polyakov told him.

"If he is an enemy of the State then most certainly it is my duty is to destroy him."

"He is my enemy," Polyakov said, after downing half the vodka in the glass.

"And because he is your enemy, he is also an enemy of the State?" Makusky questioned.

"That is what I'd want you to accept," Polyakov said.

"The comrade admiral in question is one of our national heroes; he has many, many powerful friends. But tell me more."

"I understand that you have tapes and film of Comrade Admiral Borodine with his American whore?"

"I might," Makusky answered.

"I want to use them against him," Polyakov said.

"I have already explored that possibility," Makusky answered. "There is nothing in either tapes or the films to bring charges against the comrade admiral."

Polyakov finished his drink and poured more vodka into the empty glass. "I have a plan," he said, "and I am willing to be very generous to the person who will execute it."

"Let me hear the plan," Makusky said.

"Alter the tapes so that the woman and the admiral are speaking Russian and show them to Borodine's wife."

"Go ahead, tell me more."

"She will be told that they were recently made and that this is only one of several affairs that Borodine has had during their marriage."

"The woman, I understand," Makusky said, "is pregnant."

Polyakov nodded. "And therefore very vulnerable," he commented. "Pregnant women are aware that their husband might be looking elsewhere for his pleasure."

"And what exactly do you hope to accomplish by this, other than ruining a marriage?"

"Ruining the man," Polyakov answered. "Borodine is very much in love with his wife and the child will cement that bond.

I want to rupture the present bond and injure the man. If I can't destroy him one way, I will do it another."

"She may miscarry as a result of seeing the film and hearing the tapes," Makusky said.

"So much the better. She will have more cause to hate him and he will have more cause to blame himself."

Makusky poured himself another drink.

"Are you interested in working with me?" Polyakov asked.

"How generous do you think you could be?" Makusky responded.

"Ten thousand rubles," Polyakov said.

"Twenty-five thousand American dollars in a Swiss bank," Makusky answered.

Polyakov's eyes went wide.

Makusky smiled, raised his glass and drank; then he said, "As such arrangements go, it is a reasonable price. It must be paid in full before anything is done."

Polyakov looked down at his glass and said, "In five days I will be leaving on another mission. Admiral Borodine will accompany me. This must be done during the time we are gone."

"Then you agree to my terms?" Makusky asked.

"Yes," Polyakov said. "The money will be deposited in your Swiss account."

Makusky smiled. "Admiral, you will open a new one. You will send me the number on the day you leave. Do not try to outfox me," Makusky said.

Polyakov shook his head.

"Good," Makusky said. "Now you can stay here and enjoy yourself with Maria, the woman with whom you were dancing, or you could leave. The choice is yours. If you choose to stay, I assure you that you will not soon forget the experience."

Polyakov hesitated. He desperately wanted to have a memorable experience with Maria. But he also knew that everything he did would be either recorded, or filmed. Probably both. "Thank you for the invitation," he finally said, "but I have a great deal of paperwork that must be done before I leave."

Makusky nodded, stood up and without saying another word, he left the table.

Polyakov waited a full five minutes before he too left the table.

The President called a meeting of the Joint Chiefs of Staff, the National Security Agency and the CIA. The meeting was held in the War Room, a large room more than thirty feet below the White House. The President occupied one end of an immense conference table, the Chiefs of Staff, Tysin and Mister Robert McCabe, head of the NSA arranged themselves equally on either side of the table. On one of the walls was a huge map of the world that could be electronically activated to show the position of every ship in every ocean and the last reported position of every foreign submarine. The positions of all American naval vessels, surface or subsurface, were marked in green or blue. At a flick of a switch the position of every aircraft could also be displayed and with another control, the President could display a video picture of a particular area on a screen that occupied the entire surface of the opposite wall. In time of war, he and the members of the JCS could watch a battle as it was taking place.

"Gentlemen," the President said, "I have received word from several different sources that the Russians are planning to seize control of that area off Antarctica where a huge reserve of oil has recently been discovered. This is being done in direct violation of our and their international agreements not to place any military forces in that area of the world." He pressed several buttons and a large map of Antarctica filled the screen and with an electronic pointer, he indicated where the troubled area was located. "We have reason to believe that several Russian ships are at this very moment attempting to set up some sort of drilling operation."

"Excuse me Mister President," General Miller, Chief of the Air Force said, "but it's winter down there and any such operation would be, if not impossible, then certainly extremely hazardous to men and equipment."

"They are doing it," the President said. "And I want to stop them before they are in a position to claim the area on the basis of having developed it."

"We don't even know where their ships are located," Mason said. "Unless we know that, how can anything be done?"

"Mister President, this is not my area of expertise," McCabe said, "but if my memory of geography is correct, that area of the ocean is probably, even on good days, the worst in the world."

"According to the best information we have," the President said, "they have already begun to do some sort of work. Tysin, just how good is your source?"

"Good enough to have some say in what happens down there," Tysin answered.

"Does that mean a command position?" Mason asked.

"I'm sorry, I cannot give a direct answer to that question."

"I think it would be foolish not to take the information seriously," General Winder of the Army said. "The question is how to deal with it."

"There is only one way to deal with it," the President said, "and that is to see if it is correct and if it is, then we must destroy their ability to complete their project."

"This time of year the use of aircraft is out of the question," the Air Force general said. "We'd probably lose more aircraft as a result of operating in bad weather than we would from enemy action."

"If the *Barracuda* were operational, she could go in and do the job," Mason said.

"That was my thought too," President commented. "But she's not operational."

"Several months away from being operational," Mason said. "She suffered severe internal damage."

"Then send another sub, or even two," McCabe said.

"What about that?" the President asked, looking at Mason.

"Submarines would have an easier time than any surface ship," he answered. "If we decide on sending submarines, we then have to decide on who commands them, who has overall command and equally as important, what kind of ships do we send?"

"I certainly wouldn't risk any of the newer types," Tysin said. "Some ships left over from World War Two —"

"They wouldn't survive down there," Mason said. "The boats must be nuclear and my suggestion would be to send one attack boat and another modified missile type."

"Modified missile type?" the President questioned.

"The missiles and their silos could be taken out, thereby making room for a small assault force of say fifty men to destroy the facility."

"Fifty men may not be sufficient for the task," the general of the Army said. "I'd recommend no less than triple that size."

"That would require three modified missile submarines," Mason said.

"How fast could the subs be modified?" the President asked.

"A month. Maybe three weeks."

"That's reasonable," the President said. "All right, go ahead and modify two. We'll have an assault force of a hundred men."

"I recommend that Boxer be given command," Tysin said.

The President was taken aback. "Did I hear correctly: you want the command to go to Boxer, Mister Tysin?"

"He's the most experienced we have in these matters," Tysin said. "Besides, he is friendly enough with the Russians to be able to think like them."

"I'll pretend I didn't hear that," the President said. "Is there anyone here against giving the command to Admiral Boxer? All right, he gets the command. Mason cut his orders as soon as possible. He can use the *Barracuda*'s crew. As for the commanders and crews of the other ships, I will leave that entirely up to you. But I would suggest you confer with Boxer before you choose any of the other captains. He may have some very strong views about whom he wants."

Mason nodded.

The President looked at the general of the Air Force, "Once our subs are down there, I want maximum air support. Whatever Boxer requests, regardless of the weather."

"The weather must be a factor," the general said.

"I want maximum support for Boxer," the President said. "Nothing less."

"I understand," the general said.

"Well, gentlemen, unless you have anything more to say on this matter, our meeting is over. Admiral Mason, will you please stay for a few minutes?"

"Certainly Mister President," Mason answered.

After everyone else left, the President said, "I want to know what you think about Boxer and this claustrophobia that he has?"

"I asked our chief psychiatrist about it and he seems to think that Boxer can control it and that it wouldn't become a factor in his ability to command."

The President nodded and said, "I just want to be reassured." Then he asked, "Have you gotten any word from the board?"

"No, they'll probably make their recommendations in about a month."

"Boxer'll be down in the Antarctic by then," the President said, "which leads me to the next point. I want this mission to be kept top secret. I don't want the Russians to know what's going on until it happens."

Mason nodded.

"You might consider suggesting to Boxer, when you speak to him about the mission, that I would like Colonel Dawson to lead one of the assault teams."

"I can tell you now Boxer won't have him," Mason said.

The President raised his eyebrows.

"May I speak frankly?"

"I'd be offended if you did not," the President said.

"Dawson is a coward. Boxer knows it and the men know it. I know Boxer well enough to know that if you stuff Dawson down his throat, he just might tell me to give the command to someone else."

"He can't do that, can he?"

"He can always resign," Mason said.

The President thought for several moments; then he asked, "Suppose Dawson goes along in a non-combatant role as my observer? Boxer can't object to that."

"It's a possibility," Mason answered.

The President stood up and said, "Men like Boxer are always a problem. They do spectacular things, but they do them in their own way and generally by their own rules."

"Maybe that's why they do them," Mason answered, getting to his feet.

The two of them walked to the door together.

"Better code name this operation," the President said.

"I was just thinking the same thing," Mason responded.

Tysin left Lori's apartment at ten P.M. He rode the elevator down, crossed the lobby, nodded to the doorman and pulling up his collar, went out on the street. His limo was two blocks away. He never allowed the driver to come anywhere near the house. He walked at a brisk pace with his head bent into the wind. He was thinking that maybe he and Lori could take a few days' vacation in Antigua, or some other island. He hated the winter!

Suddenly Tysin realized there was someone behind him. Someone keeping an exact distance between them. He knew he was being followed. "And it's probably not the first time either," he whispered.

That the Russians knew about his relationship with Lori scarcely made him feel uncomfortable. In the back of his mind, he knew they'd find out about it sooner or later. But he also knew that whatever information they had, they would keep secret.

Tysin turned the corner and a few moments later entered the limo. "Take me to the Washington Yacht Club," he said, looking through the rear window at an empty street. "But first drive around the corner."

"It seems to be getting colder," the driver commented.

Tysin didn't respond.

They moved around the block. Tysin checked both sides of the street and came up with nothing. The streets were deserted. He leaned back and closed his eyes. He was going to meet Julio Sanchez.

Tysin never liked Sanchez and he was sure that Sanchez felt the same way about him. He sat opposite him at a small table near the window overlooking the marina, where Sanchez's new motor yacht, the *Sea Spray*, was moored.

"If you're interested," Tysin said, "I have an assignment for you."

Sanchez gave him a broad smile. "I don't do business without first going through the prelims," he told Tysin and signaling the waiter, he said, "I'll have the usual, Bob, and my friend will have —"

"Chivas on the rocks," Tysin said.

"And Bob, bring some munchies," Sanchez said. "You know the kind I like."

"I sure do," Bob answered.

"Well, I'm glad that's out of the way," Sanchez commented. "He looked at his gold Rolex. "Eleven, would you believe I always get hungry around this time?"

"I believe it," Tysin said.

Bob returned to the table with a tray of hors d'oeuvres. "I think you'll like these, Mister Sanchez," he said. "I told the man in the kitchen to go extra heavy on the anchovies."

Sanchez nodded.

"I'll be back with the drinks in a flash," Bob said.

Tysin was anxious to get to the reason why he asked Sanchez to meet him.

"You look tired," Sanchez commented. "I think you must be working too hard. You should take it easy, man. Easy."

"If I had your money," Tysin answered, "that's exactly what I'd do."

"Ah, do I detect a bit of hostility, or is it that green-eyed monster jealousy?"

"Look, Sanchez," Tysin started, but he was interrupted by Bob's arrival with the drinks.

Sanchez raised his glass, "To whatever brought you here."

Tysin touched his glass to Sanchez's and then drank.

"Boxer gave some performance at the hearing," Sanchez said. "Even better than he gave for the hearing when my yacht accidentally rammed the *Sting Ray*."

"Boxer is the reason why I'm here," Tysin said, taking advantage of the opening Sanchez had given him.

"Boxer, Boxer," Sanchez repeated; then he said, "He and I had a falling out. Too bad, I really liked him. He's very smart and very brave."

"I want to destroy him," Tysin said tightly.

Sanchez picked up a small round cracker, topped with cheese and crowned with a rolled anchovy. "I love them," he commented with a smile; then the smile left his face and he said, "I had a falling out with the man that's all. That's not enough to kill him."

"Who said anything about killing him?" Tysin asked.

"I thought you said you want to destroy him."

"That's right. But there are many ways of doing that. I want to get at him through the woman he's living with, Francine Wheeler."

"I used to screw her," Sanchez said matter-of-factly.

"Get rid of her," Tysin said in a hard voice. "Sell her to your Arab friends."

Sanchez nodded. "That certainly would make up for the deal Boxer wrecked," he said. "But I want some extra juice, since now it's you who wants it done."

"How much do you think she'd bring?" Tysin asked.

"She's no longer prime. Probably ten, fifteen grand tops."

"And fifteen from me," Tysin said.

"When do you want this done?" Sanchez asked.

"Boxer will be leaving this country soon. I'll contact you and tell you when to pick her up. Is it a deal?"

"It's a deal," Sanchez said, offering his hand.

Tysin shook it.

# CHAPTER 10

Borodine was at the COMOMP. "All systems green," he said.

"Water temperature thirty-eight degrees," Viktor reported.

"Roger that," Borodine responded. He looked at the UWIS display of the iceberg. It was fifteen hundred feet long and four hundred feet wide. Its extreme bottom, measured by sonar, was at its deepest five hundred feet. But its average depth was three hundred feet.

"Have you radioed the base that we're approaching it?" Polyakov asked. He was standing off to the left of Borodine and looking at the UWIS display.

"Yes, Comrade Admiral," Borodine answered. He had kept relations between them formal.

The COMMO keyed Borodine, "Comrade Admiral, the captain of the supply ship *Riga* wants to speak with Comrade Admiral Polyakov."

"Patch him through," Borodine answered; then half turning toward Polyakov, he said, "Captain Garskivich wants to speak with you, Comrade Admiral."

"Comrade Garskivich, are you on?" Polyakov asked. A burst of static filled the bridge.

"Heavy —"

"I can't hear him," Polyakov complained. "Say again. Say again."

"Weather damaged —"

"Can't we get better reception?" Polyakov asked.

"Not in these latitudes," Borodine answered.

"Forced to turn back. Must have rudder —" Another burst of static gobbled up what Garskivich said.

Polyakov shouted, "I can't understand you. Say again. Say again." He looked helplessly at Borodine. "I can't make out what he's saying."

"Keep trying," Borodine told him.

Polyakov nodded and said, "Say again… Say again."

"Rudder damaged," Garskivich said, his voice suddenly coming in loud and clear. "Must repair before proceeding."

"But we need the supplies," Polyakov said. "It will be several weeks before you can return."

"The rudder is jury-rigged," Garskivich said. "I cannot risk going farther south with it. The sea is very rough and it is difficult to control —"

"Continue on your present course," Polyakov said. "A tow will be sent."

"I must have —"

"Continue on your present course," Polyakov said. "A tow will be sent… Out." He switched the radio off. "We must have those supplies," he said.

Borodine said nothing. He was well aware of the *Riga*'s importance. The ship not only carried supplies and half of the heavy construction equipment that would be needed to complete the base, but it also carried two hundred convicts, who were pulled from the various gulags to do the actual construction. Without the convict labor, the base could not be built.

Polyakov began to pace. "We need those supplies and we need the convicts it carries," he said, "or nothing more can be done."

"The one ocean-going tug we have must stay with the Ice Castle," Borodine said, referring to the base by its code name.

"And the *Volga*," Polyakov said, referring to the other supply ship, "is at least three days behind the *Riga*."

Borodine acknowledged what Polyakov said with a silent nod.

"I have no choice, I must send the *Sea Dragon*," Polyakov said.

Borodine was not surprised by Polyakov's decision. Indeed, it was the only one he could make.

"As soon as I and my aides are ashore you will rendezvous with the *Riga* and take her in tow," Polyakov said.

"The *Sea Dragon* was not built for that kind of work," Borodine responded calmly.

"She certainly has the power to do it," Polyakov answered. "As you tow, the *Riga* would probably make better time than if she were under her own power."

"That's probably true," Borodine admitted. "But we might be doing untold damage to the *Sea Dragon*'s hull. The stress in a heavy sea would be enormous and the results unknown until something happened."

"My order stands," Polyakov said. "I have no other way of bringing the *Riga* here."

"Aye, aye, Comrade Captain," Borodine answered. "But just for the record, I object to your order."

Polyakov nodded and walked swiftly off the bridge.

Borodine rubbed his beard; then turning to Viktor, he said, "The truth is that he doesn't have any other way of bringing the *Riga* in."

"The truth is also that we weren't designed or built to tow a twenty-five-thousand ton fully loaded freighter in seas where the waves average eight to fifteen feet and that might be considered a calm day."

With his hands, Borodine made a gesture of helplessness and turned his attention to the UWIS display.

The COMMO keyed Borodine. "Ice Castle acknowledges our transmission. Suggest we surface on the south side. The tug *Litniov* will be standing by... Wind southeast, thirty knots... Light snow showers... Fifty percent visibility... Air temperature twenty-four degrees below zero."

"Roger that," Borodine answered and he repeated the surface conditions to Viktor.

"We'll be iced as soon as we surface," Viktor said.

"Arrange for ice chopping details," Borodine responded. "They might as well get some practice before we begin towing the *Riga*, because then every man will have to take his turn clearing the ice topside, or we just might heel over."

"Aye, aye," Viktor answered.

Borodine keyed the SO. "Have you got an accurate range on the target?" he asked.

"Twelve thousand yards," the SO answered.

"Roger that," Borodine said. "Let me know when we come up to five thousand yards."

"Aye, aye, Comrade Admiral," the SO said.

Borodine leaned back in his swivel chair. The voyage from Kronstadt had been totally routine. Once the *Sea Dragon* cleared the harbor she dove to a hundred feet and maintained that depth until she was out in the Atlantic, where Borodine took her down to four hundred feet and maintained that depth for the next fifteen days until she rendezvoused with the supply ships; then she maintained an operating depth of two hundred feet, which was her present depth.

Viktor walked over to the COMCOMP. "Would it be possible to use some of the convicts to chop ice?" he asked.

"Probably. But it might be one hell of a problem to transfer them from the *Riga* to us."

"Probably impossible with a heavy sea running," Viktor said. "It was just a thought —"

Suddenly the SO keyed Borodine. "Multiple targets… Three… Bearing two-five degrees… Can't range them… Speed ten knots… Can't ID them either."

"Roger that," Boxer said, switching on the sonar display. "Whales," he announced, after studying it for a few moments and pointing to it, he said to Viktor, "the pattern is too irregular for it to be anything else."

Viktor bent close to the scope. "Could it be a mother and two calves," he said.

Borodine keyed the SO. "Just whales," he said.

The SO apologized.

"Better to be sorry than dead," Borodine responded.

"Aye, aye, Comrade Admiral," the SO said.

Viktor stood erect. "They are certainly wonderful creatures," he commented. "I read somewhere that they communicate to each other using a whole range of sounds and they can do it over thousands of miles."

"I read the same thing," Borodine said, suddenly aware of Polyakov's presence by the woody scent of the cologne he wore.

"Comrade Admiral," Polyakov said, "I would like to have a word with you in private."

"Viktor, take the CONN," Borodine ordered; then looking at Polyakov, he asked, "Your cabin?"

Polyakov nodded.

"Mind if I stop for coffee?" Borodine asked.

"No. I'd like a cup, too," Polyakov said.

They stopped at the mess area and from a large urn, each of them poured a cup of coffee for himself. Neither of them spoke and Polyakov led the way from the mess area to his cabin, which was directly across the passageway from Borodine's.

"Please sit down, Comrade Admiral," Polyakov said, gesturing to one of the two chairs.

Borodine sat down, took the plastic cover off the container and began to sip at the coffee.

Polyakov settled in the other chair. "I must have the *Riga* here," he said, raising the container to his lips. "Nothing can be done without the cargo she brings and the laborers."

"I'm aware of that," Borodine answered. "But I am also aware of what the *Sea Dragon* can and cannot do. Nothing might happen to her; but should it, neither I or any of my crew would be alive to complain about it."

Polyakov put the container down on the desk. "Bring the *Riga* in," he said, "and I promise that I will not interfere with you. You will be able to operate freely."

"I intended to operate freely, with or without your consent, Admiral," Borodine told him.

Polyakov laced his fingers. "I never had any doubt that you wouldn't," he said. "But —"

"Comrade Admiral, I will bring the *Riga* here," Borodine said. "I know you can't send the tug for her. Is there anything else?"

"Nothing," Polyakov answered.

Suddenly the SO keyed Borodine. "Comrade Admiral, we've reached a range of five thousand yards."

"Roger that," Borodine answered; then to Polyakov, he said, "We'll be surfacing in approximately five minutes. Every man will be needed to chop ice."

"You really don't expect me to —"

Borodine nodded. "But I do, Comrade Admiral. I certainly do. I and all the other officers will spend time on the ice chopping detail."

"In that case," Polyakov said, "so will I."

Borodine nodded, stood up and said, "Make sure you dress warmly, Comrade Admiral. The temperature is twenty below zero and the wind is thirty-five miles an hour." Then he left the cabin and hurried to the bridge. "I have the CONN," he said, coming alongside Viktor.

"All systems green," Viktor reported.

Borodine nodded and switching on the MC, he said, "All hands now hear this... All hands now hear this... This is the captain... In a matter of minutes we will be surfacing... Those men assigned to ice chopping will make sure the bridge is clear of ice first... The deck detail will clear the forward and aft diving planes... Everyone on board will take his turn at ice chopping... The boat must be kept free of ice... Until further notice, all section chiefs will rotate men every fifteen minutes... That is all." Then he keyed the DO. "Going to manual control," he said.

"Ten-four... Indication reads manual," the DO answered.

Borodine touched the klaxon button once.

Almost immediately air was fed into the ballast tanks.

Borodine keyed the DO. "Zero-three degrees on forward and after diving planes."

"Forward diving planes at zero-three degrees... Aft diving planes at zero-three degrees," the DO said.

Borodine checked the DDRO against the Depth Gauge. The *Sea Dragon* was up fifty feet. He keyed the EO. "Reduce speed to one-zero knots," he said.

"Reducing speed to one-zero knots," the EO said.

Borodine keyed the DO. "Hold at seven-five feet," he said.

"Hold at seventy-five feet," the DO responded.

Borodine gave the necessary orders to the helmsman to approach the Ice Castle from the south; then he keyed the DO. "Take her to the surface," he said.

"Going to the surface," the DO responded.

Borodine watched the DIVCON lights change from red to amber and at the same instant they went to green and began flashing, a bell began to ring. He switched on the MC. "Surface," he said. "Surface… Bridge detail top side… Deck detail topside."

"All systems green," Viktor reported.

Borodine keyed the RO. "Are you operational?" he asked.

"Surface to air radar operational," the RO answered. "Surface to surface operational… Multi surface target acquisition radar not operational."

"Get it operational," Borodine barked.

A blast of frigid air rushed through the *Sea Dragon*.

"Bridge detail in place," Viktor reported.

"Roger that," Borodine answered.

"Deck detail in place," Viktor reported.

"Take the CONN," Borodine said. "We'll try and control from the topside bridge."

"Good luck," Viktor answered.

Borodine put on his windproof jacket, gloves and face mask; then he hurried up to the bridge. The wind slammed into him, taking his breath away.

"Is that where we're going, Comrade Admiral?" A man asked from behind a face mask.

"Yes," he shouted in order to be heard over the sound of the wind. He looked down at the deck. Ice was forming almost as fast as it was being chopped away. He keyed the COMMO. "Send a message to the Ice Castle. Tell them we're on their south side and will be coming in to tie up. Tell them I need some lights to bring me in."

"Ten-four," the COMMO answered.

Borodine keyed Viktor. "I have the CONN," he said.

"How is it up there?"

"Come topside and see for yourself," Borodine answered.

The COMMO keyed Borodine. "Comrade Admiral, starting in two minutes you will have flares every two minutes."

"Roger that," Borodine answered, aware that the *Sea Dragon* was moving on a vector resulting from its course and the direction of the wind. To correct it, he keyed the EO and asked for thirty knots.

"Going to three-zero knots," the EO said.

Viktor scrambled up through the hatchway.

"How do you like this world?" Borodine asked, looking at the masked face.

"Not much, if first impressions count for anything," Viktor answered.

Suddenly a flare exploded and illuminated the mass of the Ice Castle.

"Helmsman come starb'd zero two degrees," Borodine said.

"Coming starb'd zero two degrees," the helmsman answered.

The COMMO keyed Borodine. "Comrade Admiral, Ice Castle wants to speak to you," he said

"Patch him through," Borodine said.

"Welcome, Comrade Admiral Borodine to you and your crew. You will find an opening five hundred feet from the east end of the Castle. It will be large enough to accommodate your ship. As soon as you are in position, we will be able to guide you into it."

"How do I get into position?" Borodine asked.

"Better head south for at least three thousand yards; then turn north and come directly at the Castle, keeping close to its eastern end. The flares will help you see the opening."

"Ten-four," Borodine answered; then to the helmsman, he said, "Come to course three-six-zero degrees."

"Coming to course three-six-zero degrees," the helmsman answered.

"I'm going down on deck to help with the ice chopping," Viktor said. "It's backbreaking work."

Borodine nodded. "I want to get us in position," he said; "then you take the CONN and I'll do my stint."

"You're more important up here," Viktor said.

"It will mean more to the men if they know I took my turn too," Borodine said.

Viktor nodded and then dropped down into the hatchway.

Borodine looked at the Castle and found himself hating it.

The RO keyed him, breaking into his thoughts. "Comrade Admiral, all radar are out."

"What?"

"All radar have malfunctioned," the RO said meekly.

Borodine swore; then asked, "How long before they're operational?"

"I cannot give an estimate," the RO answered. "They were working up until three minutes ago; then all of a sudden I have a malfunction signal."

"Where?"

"The main drive unit."

"On all?"

"On all," the RO repeated.

"Report as soon as they are operational," Borodine snapped. He was counting on a radar fix to determine when to change course. Now he'd have to make a visual estimate.

"Ten-four," the RO said.

The SO keyed Borodine. "Three targets, bearing, eight-four degrees... Range, twenty-four thousand yards... Speed, two-eight knots... Depth, four-five zero feet... Unable to ID."

Borodine brushed the snow off the sonar display tube and turned it on. Ordinarily whatever the SO was looking at would instantly come up on the screen. But now there were only faint green markings. Nothing that could be identified. "My screen is down. Are you sure they're not whales?" Borodine asked, over the still open key.

"I am not sure," the SO answered.

"How many targets?"

"Three."

"Same number as before."

"Yes, Comrade Admiral," the SO said.

"Are their movements the same?"

"The resolution at that distance has gotten worse," the SO explained.

"Keep tracking them," Borodine ordered.

"Aye, aye, Comrade Admiral," the SO answered.

Borodine told the helmsman to, "come to course one-eight degrees."

"Coming to course one-eight degrees," the helmsman answered.

Borodine keyed the EO. "Reduce speed to zero-eight knots."

"Reducing speed to zero-eight knots," the helmsman said.

The Castle came closer and closer and under the white magnesium light of the flares it looked whiter than anything Borodine had ever seen. Then suddenly, even as he was thinking about the intense whiteness, the flares went out.

The COMMO keyed Borodine. "Comrade Admiral, the commander of the Castle wants to speak with you."

"Patch him through," Borodine said.

"My sonar officer has ID'd three American type submarines," the commander said, "bearing, eight-four degrees... Range, twenty-four thousand yards... Speed, twenty-eight knots... Depth, four-five feet... Course, one-seven-six degrees... They are heading toward us, Comrade Admiral."

"Roger that," Borodine answered; then he asked, "Can you ID any of them?"

"Negative," the commander of the Castle responded. Borodine reached down and to the side for the klaxon button and pressed it three times. The *Sea Dragon* was crash diving.

Boxer sat at the COMCOMP and peered intently at the three-dimensional sonar display. Suddenly the ship was filled with the pinging sound of Russian sonar.

Boxer keyed the Electronics Officer. "Activate ECM," he said calmly.

"ECM activated," the EO answered.

Boxer gave his full attention to the image on the screen. There was no doubt about it: the *Sea Dragon* was maneuvering around the huge iceberg. He leaned away from the screen and pointing to it, he said to his EXO, "What do you make of it?"

Commander Mark Clemens, his new Executive Officer, was a rangy built thirty-two-year-old man, with light brown hair, a freckled face and hands, whom Boxer called Clem, or Mister Clem.

Clemens studied the screen for several moments then he said, "Either the ship's captain likes icebergs, or he's trying to land some men on it, or, and this is way out, he might be looking for a way into it." He had a distinct New England accent and a wry sense of humor.

Boxer suppressed a smile. He hadn't revealed the nature of the mission to any member of his crew, or to Commanders William Holt and Harry Banks, the captains of the two other submarines. Both had been officers aboard the *Barracuda* and despite Mason's insistence that he be allowed choose them, in the end they were Boxer's choice.

"Maybe all three," he said.

The COMMO keyed Boxer. "Skipper, increased radio traffic."

"Roger that," Boxer said; then he added, "Send the following message to Pig One and Two. Move east another ten thousand yards... Surface... Captains and EXO's stand by to board command boat... Send this code ten... No response necessary."

Aye, aye, Skipper," the COMMO answered.

Mahony, come to seven-four degrees," Boxer said.

"Coming to seven-four degrees," the helmsman answered.

Boxer glanced up at Clemens, and said, "Well Clem, you'll soon find out why we're down here."

"If it's what I think it is, I'd rather hold on to my dream of towing an iceberg to wherever icebergs are towed to."

"You can absent yourself from the meeting and find out later," Boxer teased.

"Skipper, I wouldn't miss this one for … for a sweet tit on a cold November afternoon."

"Then as the man said, 'be there!'" Boxer said.

"Level at three hundred feet," the DO said.

"Roger that," Borodine answered and keyed the COMMO. "Contact the Castle —"

"The commander is already on the radio, Comrade Admiral," the COMMO said.

"Patch him through."

"Aye, aye, Comrade Admiral," the COMMO answered.

"We have lost contact with the targets," the commander said. "But from the tapes we made, we were able to ID one of the ships... An attack submarine of the Wahoo class... The other two ships are unknown."

"Roger that," Borodine answered, silently pleased that he wouldn't have to face Boxer again.

"Comrade Admiral, the question now is what do we do?" the commander asked.

"As quickly as possible, I put ashore Comrade Admiral Polyakov, who is the Castle's over-all commander, and half my assault team. How many combat ready troops do you have?"

"None... All our personnel are construction types, technical or administrative. And we have a convict complement of one hundred men. But half of those are sick and dying."

Borodine suddenly remembered the convicts aboard the *Riga* and realized that they were being sent to replace those who had already died and those who were dying. He turned to Polyakov, who was standing directly behind him. "There aren't any combat troops in the Castle," he said.

"Then you must land your entire force," Polyakov answered.

Borodine nodded. "I will land my entire assault team. Have you the necessary provisions to feed them and the necessary areas to house them?"

"Yes. This facility is almost complete. The power plant goes into operation within the next two days and at that time we will be capable of moving at a speed of ten knots."

"Keep the sonar operational on a twenty-four hour basis," Borodine said. "We are going to surface and land... Stand by... I need light in order to make my approach... I will radio when I am approximately five hundred yards away… I want flares up every two minutes until I am safely inside the tunnel."

"Aye, aye, Comrade Admiral," the commander responded.

Borodine signaled to Viktor. "You have the CONN… Take her up… Same situation as before… Ice chopping details to work in ten-minute shifts… I'll be on the bridge shortly after we surface."

"Aye, aye," Viktor answered, sitting down at the COMCOMP.

Borodine motioned to Polyakov and said, "I want to talk to you, Comrade Admiral. We can use the mess area." And he took the lead.

Polyakov caught up with him and started to say something, but Borodine said, "Not until we're seated in the mess area."

A few minutes later they sat opposite each other. Borodine had a mug of black coffee in front of him and a piece of freshly made blueberry pie. Polyakov drank tea with milk from a glass.

Borodine put his fork down and looking straight at Polyakov, he said, "I want you to know exactly where I stand."

"I think I do," Polyakov answered.

"Your thinking is often fuzzy," Borodine told him.

"I don't have to take —"

"Sit down," Borodine snapped. "Aboard the ship, you may outrank me, but I give the orders. I want you to keep this in your mind: if any of my men are killed because of your stupidity, I will kill you." Borodine spoke in a flat voice. "I will not bring you up on charges. I will kill you myself. Do you understand that?"

Polyakov turned pale.

"More than understand it, do you believe it?"

Polyakov nodded.

"Not good enough," Borodine said, "I want to hear it from your own lips."

"I believe it," Polyakov answered in a low voice.

"Good. Now, there are several other things I want you to understand," Borodine said, aware that the bow of the *Sea Dragon* was up. "You will command this base, but with my approval. Any decision of a military nature, I will make. You can decide anything else. But I will make all the military decisions."

"That can't be!" Polyakov exclaimed, starting to stand.

Borodine reached across the table and pushed him down. "I will not give the orders. You will. But you will not give them unless I approve."

"And if I don't choose to follow —"

"You're dead," Borodine said. "Any member of the assault team would be more than willing to use a bullet, or a knife. Polyakov, don't be a fool. Your face will be saved."

After several moments of silence, Polyakov nodded and asked stiffly, "Is there anything else?"

"Order the *Riga* to find a port where she could be repaired," Borodine said.

"But we need the supplies," Polyakov said.

"There are three American submarines out there. What chance do you think the *Riga* would have against them?"

"Very little," Polyakov admitted.

"There's one more thing," Borodine told him. "I haven't seen the condition in which the convicts are forced to live, but I have a very good idea of what they're like. You're going to issue orders to improve them."

"That's not a military decision," Polyakov objected. "It is not in your self-proscribed domain."

"Those convicts might have to be armed —"

"Are you insane?"

"Polyakov, use the brain nature so generously gave you and which you continually misuse. There are three American subs out there. One of them is an attack type. Old, yes, but still very deadly and probably refitted with new electronic devices, to say nothing of new weapons. Now, what do you think the other ships are there for?"

"An attack force," Polyakov answered.

"Good," Borodine said and gesturing with his hand, he added, "Now give me the rest of it. Come… Come… Ah, you disappoint me, Admiral. I thought you put it all together. Let me do it for you, they're troop-carrying ships."

"You can't know that!"

"I will bet you a month's pay that when we ID them, they'll be large enough to carry an assault force."

"Then they mean to attack the Castle?"

Borodine nodded. "I'm sure they will try."

"But how could the Americans have found out about it?" Polyakov questioned.

"The same way we find out about their secret operations," Borodine said, finishing his pie and coffee.

Suddenly the klaxon sounded.

"We're at the surface," Borodine said, getting to his feet. "I'll be needed on the bridge. I feel much better about things, now that we've had our little talk. You should too, because now you know exactly where you stand."

Polyakov didn't answer.

Holt, Banks and the EXOs, Norris and Fields and Clemens were squeezed into Boxer's small cabin. Holt and Banks sat on the bunk bed; Norris and Fields stood against one of the walls. Clemens stood at the door. Boxer was the only one seated.

"I don't advise smoking," Boxer said, "unless you have some unique way of venting this place. I'm going to make this short and sweet, or this boat will roll itself to death. Our objective is to destroy an iceberg that the Russians have turned into a fortress. We'll move in immediately. The sooner we get it over with, the quicker we can get the hell out of this place." He spread a map of the Southern Ocean across the top of his desk. "The red circle is where we are," he said. "A hundred or so miles south of us begins the ice fields. The American bases are circled in blue. You can see that we're a good five hundred miles from the nearest one. Although I was promised air support, I don't think we can count on it. At least not now, when we need it. According to our MET officer, there's a storm system coming in within the next twelve hours. We're going to use that for cover. Harry, Bill, I want your assault troops on the berg as soon as possible. I'm going to draw Comrade Borodine away from the base. That will give you an opportunity to go in unopposed. But you can expect opposition on the berg. So far, are there any questions?"

"Have we any idea where the entrance is?" Holt asked.

"None. Major Williams will have overall command ashore," Boxer said. "Banks, you tell him not to waste any time. Destroy anything that looks remotely usable."

"Will do, Skipper," Banks answered.

"How much opposition can our men expect?" Clemens asked.

"As much as Comrade Borodine's assault force can give," Boxer answered. "My guess is that his men are the only combat ready troops on the berg. I don't think the Russians put a combat force on it."

"His force numbers a hundred and fifty," Banks said.

"To the man," Boxer answered.

"We'll be going in short."

"But with luck, surprise will be on our side," Boxer answered.

"What happens after the facility is destroyed?" Holt asked. "Do we take prisoners?"

"You disarm any of the men left and send a distress signal. It will be answered from one of the Russian bases. They should be able to get here in plenty of time."

"When do we return for our assault troops?" Holt asked.

"As soon as Williams signals that it is safe for you to return," Boxer answered. "I want you to lay off the berg about ten thousand yards so you can get in and out in a hurry. As soon as your men are aboard, head north as fast as you can. Get out of here and back to the States. With any luck you should be on your way home in about seven to eight hours."

"Sounds too easy," Banks said.

"It just sounds that way," Boxer answered. "The weather is going to make it seem more like hell than anything else." He looked at his watch. "In exactly forty-five minutes I'll be moving into position. My plan is to fire a torpedo and do a bit of damage that way. It should be enough to bring Comrade Borodine out."

"You can't outrun him in this boat," Holt said.

"I'm not planning to try," Boxer said. "I just want to draw him away from the berg and give you guys a chance to get in and out without having to face the *Sea Dragon*."

Holt and Banks looked at one another; then Banks said, "Skipper, each of us have four surface-to-surface missiles left. We can coordinate and you can fire them from this ship."

"Mister Clem, will you see that our FCO plugs into the FC computers of the Pigs," Boxer said.

Clemens nodded.

"Any other questions, comments or suggestions?" Boxer asked. "None… Okay men, I have thirteen hundred. That front will be here by nineteen hundred. I'll move toward the berg forty-five minutes after we disperse."

Clemens stepped aside, squeezed close to the wall and managed to open the door.

"Good luck," Boxer said, as the men filed out of the cabin.

# CHAPTER 11

Boxer drove the ship close to the bottom, a depth of five hundred feet, and moved very slowly toward the iceberg. Unlike the *Barracuda*, this boat, which he nicknamed *Tiny Tim*, lacked some of the electronic gear he was used to using. Though fitted with the UWIS, the equipment only had a five-thousand yard range and its sonar had a maximum operating range of fifteen thousand yards. Because it was an attack submarine, its armament consisted of six torpedo tubes: four forward and two aft. For this mission, it was fitted with two batteries of four killer darts each. It completely lacked any sort of missile firing capability. There just wasn't any place aboard where the necessary fire control computers could be put without having to sacrifice something else.

The ship had a crew of a hundred and twenty-five officers and men, all of whom came from the *Barracuda*, with the exception of Clemens, who wrote directly to Boxer and asked to be considered for the crew of the *Barracuda*. Boxer met with him, liked his style and after checking his record, assigned him to be his EXO for this particular mission.

"Ambient water temperature three-eight degrees," Clemens reported.

"No differentials to hide in," Boxer answered. They were working so close that either one of them could reach out and touch the other.

"The surface is exactly one degree warmer," Clemens said.

Boxer checked his control panel. They still weren't in sonar range of the berg.

"What do you think the assault team will find?" Clemens asked.

"Enough to make it worthwhile to blow it," Boxer said, looking toward the bow and then the stern. In either direction he could see the sections at their battle stations. Ordinarily, those men not on duty were either in the small mess area, or their bunks asleep. Bunks were shared by at least two, sometimes three men. The men slept, ate and worked in shifts.

The SO keyed Boxer. "Target, bearing two-six-five degrees, range, five thousand yards… Dead in the water… No ID."

"Roger that," Boxer answered and keyed the EO, "Reduce speed to zero-seven knots"

"Reducing speed to zero-seven knots," the EO said.

Boxer turned on the UWIS. "Now for a bottom view of the iceberg," he said and began adjusting the optical scan equipment to sharpen the image created by sonar digital image. "Take a look-see," he said, bending away to let Clemens move closer to the screen.

"Looks like a moonscape turned upside down," Clemens said. "It's really very beautiful."

"And we're seeing it without any light on it," Boxer said. "The UWIS creates artificial light for the image on the screen."

Clemens moved back to his station. "Maybe someday I'll paint it," he commented, more to himself than to Boxer.

"A good friend of mine was a painter," Boxer said, remembering that a long time ago he had looked at some of Captain Rugger's paintings in the cabin of the *Tecumseh*.

"Was? Isn't he still?"

"He was killed," Boxer said.

"On a mission?" Clemens questioned after a few moments of silence.

"It's a long story," Boxer said. "I still have some of his paintings. Most of them are in storage. But I have one large one at home and a dozen or so drawings and pastels he did."

"I'd like to see them someday," Clemens responded.

Boxer nodded. "Maybe someday," he said, knowing he would never show the nude of Francine, or any of the nude drawings Rugger had done of her to him. Suddenly he was filled with an enormous longing to be with her.

"If I hadn't become an officer, I might have wound up a starving artist."

"Are you any good?" Boxer asked, realizing the two of them were having an ordinary conversation in extraordinary circumstances. As long as he had known Cowly, he had never had a similar conversation with him.

The COMMO keyed Boxer. "High priority Russian radio traffic," he said.

"Roger that," Boxer acknowledged; then he said, "You can bet they're talking about us."

"Not in very complimentary terms, I'd be willing to bet," Clemens said.

Suddenly a red light on the COMCOMP began to flash. "Their sonar is searching for us." He keyed the ELO. "I have a SDS."

"Came up on my board too," the ELO said. "The sector indicator isn't holding steady… Best guess is that it's searching between three-eight degrees and seven-zero degrees."

"Beam pattern?"

"Cone shaped," the ELO answered.

"If it starts moving toward seven-five degrees let me know," Boxer said.

"Aye, aye, Skipper," the ELO responded.

Boxer checked the UWIS. The bottom of the iceberg was more sharply defined. "Now look at the sucker," Boxer said, pointing to the UWIS screen.

Clemens came close again. "Skipper, there's something below it," he said and stepped back.

"A pod of some sort," Boxer commented, looking at the screen again. "Probably it's a sonar transducer."

"If we could knock that out," Clemens said, "then the Pigs would be able to get in without being detected and it might give us a bit of an edge too."

"It won't do anything for us," Boxer answered, "but it will help the Pigs." He keyed the FCO. "I have a visual display of the target on the UWIS… Prepare for Fire Mission."

"Aye, aye, Skipper," the FCO said. "FC COMP using UWIS coordinates… Range thirty-five hundred yards… Tracking, target dead in the water."

"Roger that," Boxer said and keyed the forward TO. "Load and arm torpedo one… Set for electronic control… FC ready."

"Ten-four, Skipper… Arming and loading torpedo one… Set for electronic control."

Boxer watched the COMCOMP. The FC COMP showed green. Two red lights came on indicating that the torpedo was armed and the guide wires were plugged into its guidance system. Within moments Torpedo Tube Indicator began to flash and the READY TO FIRE message came up on the FC scope.

Boxer keyed the TO. "Stand by to fire," he said.

"Standing by," the TO answered.

Boxer keyed the FCO. "Signal green," he said.

"Signal green," the FCO repeated.

"Data feeding," Boxer said.

"Check," Clemens answered.

Boxer touched the red Fire Control button on the COMCOMP. The hissing sound of escaping high-pressure air filled the boat.

The FTO keyed Boxer. "Fish away."

"Roger that," Boxer answered; then looking over at Mahony, he said, "Come to course four-eight degrees."

"Coming to course four-eight degrees," Mahony answered.

Boxer keyed the EO. "Flank speed," he said.

"Flank speed," the EO answered.

Boxer eyed the Time To Target Clock. The seconds jerked by.

The FCO keyed Boxer. "No change in target's position," he said.

"Roger that," Boxer answered, his eyes on the TTTC. "Now!" he exclaimed and the dull boom of an explosion sounded through the ship; then became louder and louder until the sound crashed all around them.

Borodine looked aft from the bridge; then forward, and over the MC, he said, "Stand by to cast off all lines." His voice had a peculiar dull sound in the long tunnel. He turned to Viktor. "I don't like it in here. It gives me the creeps."

Viktor looked up at the brilliantly lit roof and walls. "I remember seeing something like this in a science fiction film," he said.

"Cast off all lines," Borodine said.

Suddenly an explosion tore across the Castle. The lights in the tunnel went out. Chunks of ice began to fall. Sirens began to wail.

Borodine swore and touched the light switch. Immediately the high intensity lights from the *Sea Dragon*'s sail stabbed through the darkness. He touched the klaxon button four times, indicating a surface emergency.

Chunks of ice were still falling. The ice piers on either side of the *Sea Dragon* were split into several pieces and there were injured on each of the sections.

"Look aft!" Viktor exclaimed.

Borodine turned. The tunnel roof had collapsed. He clenched his jaw and over the MC, he said, "All hands, stand by... Condition red... Condition red!"

The COMMO keyed him. "Comrade Admiral, Comrade Admiral Polyakov is on the radio."

"Patch him through," Borodine said.

"Comrade Admiral," Polyakov said, "damage has been severe. At least fifty dead and many more casualties."

"Roger that," Borodine answered.

"You must stay and help," Polyakov said.

"Negative," Borodine said. "That explosion was caused by a torpedo. I've got to get my boat out of here, or none of us will survive."

For a few moments Polyakov was silent; then he asked, "That's your decision?"

"Roger that," Borodine answered and switched off the radio. "Stand by to dive," he announced over the MC. "All hands stand by to dive!" He pressed the klaxon three times, secured the COMCOMP and following Viktor, he scrambled down the hatchway, dogging it shut behind him.

Boxer switched on the MC. "All hands... All hands stand by for shock wave... Stand by for shock wave!"

Suddenly the *Tiny Tim* was slammed down on the bottom and bounced up again.

"Christ!" Boxer swore.

It bumped down again and scraped along the bottom for a dozen yards before it rose to its former depth.

Boxer keyed the DCO. "Anything?" he asked.

"Nothing showing up on the SYSCHEK," the DCO answered. "But I wouldn't bet on anything else."

"Roger that," Boxer answered. He wouldn't bet on it either.

"Six-two-five feet," the DO reported.

"Roger that," Borodine said, checking the UWIS. They were well below the bottom of the Castle. He keyed the EO. "Two-zero knots," he ordered.

"Two-zero knots," the EO answered.

Borodine checked the sonar display. "That boat has to be close by," he growled.

Suddenly, the sonar display flashed red.

The SO keyed Borodine. "Target, bearing, four-four degrees... Range, five thousand yards... Speed, two-four knots... Depth, four-five feet... Course, six-three degrees... ID, Wahoo attack class, recently modified."

"Roger that," Borodine answered, training the UWIS on it and bringing it into sharp focus, he keyed the FCO, "Lock FC COMP on sonar input."

"Locking FC COMP on sonar input data," the FCO answered.

Borodine keyed the FTO. "Load and arm for tubes one and two."

"Loading and arming for tubes one and two," the FTO answered.

Borodine checked the FC section of the COMCOMP. All data was being fed into the navigational computer of each of the torpedoes.

The FTO keyed Borodine, "Torpedoes loaded and ready to fire."

The red firing signal light began to flash.

The SO keyed him, "Target off screen," he reported.

Borodine's went to the sonar display. The red light stopped flashing. "What the hell happened to it?" he shouted.

"It —"

"Never mind," Borodine said. "Keep searching for it."

"Aye, aye, Comrade Admiral," the SO answered.

Borodine keyed the FCO and the FTO. "Torpedo firing holding at minus fifteen seconds," he said, knowing that if the sequence had gone for another five seconds, the torpedoes would have been fired automatically.

Both officers acknowledged the change.

"That fucking ship is still on the UWIS," Borodine said. "If I could get my firing data from it, I'd have a kill." He ran his hand over his beard. Suddenly he realized he was looking at a torpedo.

The SO keyed him, "Two targets, bearing six-one degrees… Range, eight thousand yards… Speed, seventy knots… ID, torpedoes… Torpedoes, closing fast."

Borodine slammed his hand against the Manual Control Override Switch and blew all ballast. "Helm hard to port," he ordered. "Hard to port." He keyed the EO. "Flank speed," he said tightly. "Go to flank speed."

The EO keyed Borodine and reported, "Torpedoes slowed."

"Roger that," Borodine acknowledged. "Could be sound seekers," he commented aloud to himself.

"How many?" Viktor asked.

"Two," Borodine answered. He keyed the EO. "Zero speed… Zero speed."

"Going to zero speed," the EO answered.

Borodine changed the position of several switches. The *Sea Dragon*'s upward movement slowed and ceased altogether.

Borodine checked the depth gauge. They were down one-seven-five feet.

"Where are they now?" Viktor asked.

"Still hunting."

"How long can they do that?" he asked.

Borodine shrugged and was about to say he didn't know when suddenly the torpedoes found their target and started toward the *Sea Dragon* again. "They're heat seekers," Borodine shouted. This time he put all systems under the control of the COMCOMP and increased the *Sea Dragon*'s speed from zero to flank.

The EO keyed Borodine and reported, "Torpedoes closing fast."

"Roger that," Borodine said. He switched on the MC, "Rig for impact… All hands rig for impact!" He stared at the UWIS and in an instant remembered his last night with Tanya… Silently he spoke her name… The torpedoes began to slow. An explosion rocked the *Sea Dragon* and a second one came moments after the first. The *Sea Dragon* shuddered and seemed unable to move forward; then it plunged ahead, dropping fifty feet before it came back to its operating depth.

Borodine ran his sleeve across his brow. "Close," he said. "That was very close." And he immediately keyed the DCO.

"Taking water in the forward torpedo room," the DCO reported. "Several seams open… All systems functioning."

"Can the seams be closed?" Borodine asked.

"Yes," the DCO said, "but I wouldn't make any deep dives until we can weld the outside. Limit the depth of your dives."

"Roger that," Borodine answered; then turning to Viktor, he said, "It could have been worse."

"We could have been at the bottom," Viktor said.

Borodine nodded and looked at the sonar display… The red target indicator was flashing.

"So far so good," Boxer said, looking at the sonar display and listening to the pinging of the *Sea Dragon*'s sonar. "Comrade Admiral Borodine is following us. Mahony, come to nine-zero degrees."

"Coming to nine-zero degrees," Mahony answered.

Boxer switched on the MC. "All systems going to AUTOCON," he said, repositioning a half dozen switches.

The COMMO keyed Boxer. "Pig One and Pig Two moving in."

"Roger that," Boxer answered. "Keep all communication channels open."

"Aye, aye, Skipper," the COMMO answered.

"Scrambler on?"

"Scrambler on," the COMMO answered.

Boxer leaned over and touched Clemens on the elbow. "Monitor the landing OP," he said, handing him a radio headset and plugging it into a jack. "Keep me posted."

"Will do," Clemens answered.

Boxer realized the man was very pale. "You all right?"

"Fine," Clemens answered with nod. "I'm just not used to all this action."

"Stick with it," Boxer said. "You don't get used to it, but manage to live with it."

The SO keyed Boxer, "Multiple targets, bearing one-four-two-degrees… Range, six thousand yards… Speed, eight-zero knots… ID, four killer darts… Closing fast."

Boxer flooded the tanks and went to flank speed. "Targets spreading out," the SO reported.

"Roger that," Boxer said, looking at the UWIS. Suddenly a red light began to flash on the Propulsion System portion of the COMCOMP.

The DCO keyed Boxer. "We're getting water in the main gearbox," he reported.

"Can you do anything about it?"

"Not while we're underway," the DCO said.

Boxer looked at the sonar display. The killer darts were close enough for him to see.

"Skipper," DCO said, "we might be able to handle it if we cut our speed."

"Can't do that now," Boxer said and he dialed five degrees on the bow and stern planes.

The *Tiny Tim* rushed toward the surface.

Boxer watched the killer darts. They were still moving toward the *Tiny Tim* and with enough of a spread between them that made it almost impossible to escape being hit.

"Landing team ashore," Clemens nodded, looking at Boxer. "Fighting heavy."

Boxer nodded.

The SO keyed Boxer. "Killer darts closing fast… Range one thousand yards."

"Roger that," Boxer answered. And he keyed the FTO. "Stand by to resume fire mission."

"Standing by," the FTO answered.

"Arm and load a torpedo for tube one… All sequences will be controlled from COMCOMP."

"Aye, aye, Skipper," the FTO answered.

Boxer watched the indicators. As soon as the torpedo was in the tube, he fed the data from the sonar into the torpedo's navigational system.

The SO keyed Boxer. "Range eight hundred yards."

"Roger that," Boxer said, setting the time, distance fuse in the torpedo to explode twenty-two seconds after firing and at a distance of five hundred yards from the *Tiny Tim*. He pressed the red fire control button. A green light began to flash, indicating the torpedo was away. Boxer looked at the UWIS. The torpedo was streaking toward the missile darts.

"Skipper," Clemens said, "Pig One's assault force has reached the reactor containment area."

Boxer did a double take. He did not expect the Russians to have been that far along.

"Pig Two —" Clemens began.

A huge explosion suddenly smashed down on the *Tiny Tim*, sending it down and then to the starboard. Boxer and Clemens were thrown to the deck. The lights went out and then came on.

Another explosion followed.

A green light flashed and a bell began to ring, indicating they had surfaced.

Mahony pulled himself up. His cheek was full of blood.

Boxer switched on the MC. "Bridge detail topside," he ordered.

Within moments a blast of frigid air rushed through the *Tiny Tim*.

Still on the MC, Boxer said, "All sections report any casualties."

"Skipper," Clemens said, "all transmission from Pig One and Pig Two has stopped."

Before Boxer could answer, the DO keyed Boxer, "Skipper, you're needed topside."

"Roger that," Boxer answered; then to Clemens, he said, "Switch to regular frequency."

Boxer checked the sonar scope. The *Sea Dragon* was off the scope. "I don't fucking believe it!" he exclaimed and grabbing his arctic gear, he hurried topside.

"There," the DO said, pointing toward where the iceberg was. "Look over there!"

A mushroom-shaped cloud rose into the night sky and below water was on fire.

"Do you believe that?" the DO asked, his voice full of awe.

The COMMO keyed Boxer. "A heavy Russian radio traffic again," he reported.

"Can you tell if it's coming from the *Sea Dragon*?"

"Too much static for that," the COMMO answered.

"Roger that," Boxer said and he keyed Clemens. "Come topside, Clem, and dress for the occasion."

"Aye, aye, Skipper," Clemens answered and added, "still no answer from Pig One and Pig Two."

"Roger that," Boxer responded.

"Is it what I think it is?" the DO asked.

Boxer nodded.

The ELO keyed Boxer. "Skipper, there's been a sudden jump in the radiation level."

"Has it reached the red zone?" Boxer asked.

"Close to it, but holding steady," the ELO answered.

"Roger that," Boxer said.

Clemens clambered up through the hatchway.

"That's why you lost contact with Pig One and Pig Two," Boxer said. "They don't exist anymore."

"My God!" Clemens exclaimed.

DCO keyed Boxer. "Skipper, we've got a couple of real serious problems."

"Go ahead, spell them out."

"We're taking water from a dozen different places in the forward torpedo area and we're losing pressure in the main propulsion system. These are new; they have nothing to do with the propulsion —"

"Give me the bottom line."

"We'll never make it home in our condition," the DCO said.

"How long do you think we can continue to operate?"

"At flank speed, I'd say about an hour. The speed will drop as the pressure drops."

"Override and reduce speed," Boxer said.

"Overriding and reducing speed to zero-six knots," the DCO said. "That should keep us moving for three to four hours."

"And we probably could get another ten to fifteen out of the emergency batteries."

"Maybe even twenty if we cut out using the juice for other things," the DCO said.

"Roger that," Boxer answered and rubbing his beard, he said to Clemens, "You bought yourself a real ticket when you came aboard."

"The guys on Pig One and Pig Two are the ones who really bought it," Clemens answered.

Boxer nodded. Looking toward the mushroom cloud, he wondered how many of his men would wish themselves dead, how many would die before they were safe again *and if — and it was an enormous if* — any of them would ever survive.

The COMMO keyed Boxer. "Skipper, the *Sea Dragon* is sending a May Day."

"Are you sure it's the *Sea Dragon*?"

"She ID'd herself."

"Raise it… I want to speak to Comrade Admiral Borodine," Boxer said. His mood suddenly changed. He was almost happy.

"Comrade Admiral Boxer," Borodine said, "I did not realize it was you —"

"Igor," Boxer said, "we don't have time to chat… My ship has been badly damaged and so has yours."

"I probably have four to five hours before I'll have to abandon her… How much time have you?"

"My DCO gives us about fifteen, maybe twenty… Rendezvous with me… We'll have a better chance of surviving if we're together than if we're alone."

"Where will we go?"

"South to where the ice shelf is. We can cross the ice shelf to the American base at McMurdo Sound, or we can hope to be picked up by one of our ships, or yours."

"It's the best chance we have," Borodine said.

"It's the only chance any of us have," Boxer answered…

# A NOTE TO THE READER

Dear Reader,

If you have enjoyed the novel enough to leave a review on **Amazon** and **Goodreads**, then we would be truly grateful.

Sapere Books

**Sapere Books** is an exciting new publisher of brilliant fiction and popular history.

To find out more about our latest releases and our monthly bargain books visit our website:
**saperebooks.com**

Printed in Great Britain
by Amazon

27395939R00145